The First Time Ever Published!

The 17th Donut Mystery

From *New York Times* Bestselling Author

Jessica Beck

OLD FASHIONED CROOKS

D1365345

Other Books by Jessica Beck

The Donut Mysteries

Glazed Murder
Fatally Frosted
Sinister Sprinkles
Evil Éclairs
Tragic Toppings
Killer Crullers
Drop Dead Chocolate
Powdered Peril
Illegally Iced
Deadly Donuts
Assault and Batter
Sweet Suspects
Deep Fried Homicide
Custard Crime
Lemon Larceny
Bad Bites
Old Fashioned Crooks

The Classic Diner Mysteries

A Chili Death
A Deadly Beef
A Killer Cake
A Baked Ham
A Bad Egg
A Real Pickle
A Burned Out Baker

The Ghost Cat Cozy Mysteries

Ghost Cat: Midnight Paws
Ghost Cat 2: Bid for Midnight

Jessica Beck is the *New York Times* Bestselling Author of the Donut Shop Mysteries, the Classic Diner Mysteries, and the Ghost Cat Cozy Mysteries.

To P and E,
my reasons why!

Chapter 1

It was originally meant to be a fun event that the entire community could enjoy, a pleasant way to spend an evening and help raise money for a good cause.

Instead, the festivities turned out to be the backdrop for murder, a homicide that found its way to my donut shop's front door on a night when I should have been home getting ready for bed instead of out and about on the suddenly perilous dark streets of my otherwise idyllic hometown of April Springs, North Carolina.

Chapter 2

"Suzanne, did Rick come in here by any chance while I was gone?" Emma Blake, my assistant, asked me when she hurried into Donut Hearts as darkness started to fall outside. It was odd being in my donut shop at the beginning of nighttime instead of the middle and end of it, but then again, this was turning out to be an unusual night in more ways than one.

"Sorry; I haven't seen him," I told her as I began rearranging the donuts we had left in the display case.

Emma frowned for a moment, and then she replied, "I don't get it. He was supposed to meet me out front ten minutes ago. It's starting to get chilly out there."

"What can I say? Maybe something distracted him. Emma, if you want to grab your coat and then go out and enjoy Spirit Night, I can handle things here on my own now that we've got things wrapped up in the kitchen. I fully realize that asking you to work at night is going above and beyond the call of duty. I still can't believe that I offered to open the donut shop this late in the day."

"How could you say no?" Emma asked. "Practically every shop in town is staying open for the festivities, even ReNEWed right next door. Besides, it's for a good cause."

"I know the school needs money for new band uniforms, but honestly, I would have rather just written them a check," I said with a smile.

"But if you had done that, then you would have missed out on all of this," she said as she gestured at the folks milling about outside. "Besides, I thought you'd welcome the distraction, you know, considering everything."

"Considering what, specifically?" I asked her as I turned to face her. I knew perfectly well what she was talking about, but I was tired of her tiptoeing around me. If she was going to say something, she needed to just come out and say it.

To her credit, at least Emma managed to look a little

uncomfortable as she spoke. "Suzanne, it's no big secret that your boyfriend is out of town again, even after you thought he was done with his job with the state police."

I took her hands in mine and smiled. "Emma, you worry too much. In the first place, Jake's not my boyfriend; he's my fiancé. In the second place, he's wrapping things up with his job. It's not his fault that his boss is making him work a full six weeks' notice. The best thing about it is that when his time is over, he'll be back here for good."

"I'm sure that you're right," Emma said. "I'd just hate to see you get disappointed."

"Are you kidding? I'm marrying the man of my dreams," I said with a grin. "It's tough to be too disappointed about that."

"How's Chief Martin feel about being drafted back into duty after he tried to quit?" Emma asked me.

"The chief understands that he needs to step up until the mayor can find a replacement for him. Until then, he's doing his job again, however grudgingly."

"And you're positive there's no way that Jake will want to take over as police chief after he leaves the state police for good?"

I shrugged. "He claims that he's done with law enforcement as a career forever, but I'm not so sure, myself. I think he'd be a perfect fit for the April Springs police department, but it's not my call. I'll be happy with whatever he decides to do."

"What if he wants you to move somewhere else?" Emma asked me, her question coming out in a rush of words. There it was. She'd finally voiced her fears that I'd close Donut Hearts the moment that Jake and I got married, and now I could address it out in the open.

"It's not going to happen," I said as I squeezed her hands. "Don't worry about me, or your job. I'm not going anywhere." I gestured around the shop as I added, "This is all too important to me to ever just walk away from it. Now, do you feel better?"

"A little bit," Emma said with a hesitant smile. "I'd be even better if I knew what Rick was up to."

"Like I said, I can't help you with that. If you're that worried about him, though, go out and see if you can find him." I looked outside to see crowds of people wandering up and down Springs Drive. Quite a few folks were wearing the high school's colors of blue and gold, but nearly an equal amount were dressed in Halloween costumes, including a great many adorned in plain white sheets with holes cut out for eyes. Apparently a lot of folks in town had decided that Spirit Night deserved its own set of ghosts, aka spirits, and they were enthusiastically joining in on the fun. In honor of the special celebration, I'd created a Band Buster Donut, a plain cake donut decorated with blue and gold stripes and topped with a dollop of whipped cream. Emma had teasingly played with the idea of calling it a Band Aid Donut, but we hadn't been sure how that name would be perceived by our customers, so we'd changed it to something a little more acceptable. On a lark, I'd also made a regular solid yeast donut, left unfilled, but covered with white icing. As a finishing embellishment, I'd even added two small round bits of chocolate to serve as eyes, and another larger one for the mouth. I could be as playful as everyone else, so I called it the Spirit Donut and put it on sale as well. They were actually doing better than the Band Busters, and I thought about adding them to our regular autumn menu. I was about to say so when I saw that Emma was completely lost in the outdoor festivities; honestly, she might as well go find her errant boyfriend. "Go. There's no reason that both of us need to hang out around here," I said.

"Are you sure?" she asked me eagerly as she grabbed her jacket. Emma was just starting the first year of her twenties, and I was grateful to have her working for me instead of off somewhere in college. My assistant took some classes at the local community college during the afternoons and evenings, but nothing that interfered with her time working with me.

Usually.

Then again, Donut Hearts wasn't usually open at seven o'clock at night.

"I'm positive," I said. "Now go before I change my mind!"

"Thanks. I'll check in with you later, just in case," Emma said happily as she headed out the door, hot on the trail of her boyfriend. I wasn't a big fan of Rick's for several reasons. For one thing, he was in his early thirties, an age I considered too old for my assistant. Added to that was the fact that I had a sneaking suspicion that she wasn't the only object of his affection. Finally, his means of support wasn't entirely clear to the casual observer, and yet he always managed to flash a wad of cash around wherever he went. I kept telling myself that it wasn't any of my business, but I'd always thought of Emma as a combination sister and daughter, and that meant that I constantly lost the argument with myself that it would be smarter to just butt out of her love life altogether. Besides, I knew that Ray and Sharon Blake, Emma's parents, weren't pleased with the relationship either, so there was no real need for me to add my voice into the mix.

That didn't mean that I was just going to let it go entirely, though.

I was still wondering if there was a subtle way that I could discourage Emma from seeing Rick when my best friend, Grace Gauge, walked in carrying a pennant on a stick. She was wearing a lovely blue coat and had a gold scarf tied fashionably around her neck. Slim and pretty, she looked more like a model than a cosmetics rep. "Go Bulldogs! Woof, woof," Grace said with a smile as she waved the flag eagerly in my direction.

"Not you, too," I said with a smile.

"Why not? After all, it's not every day that April Springs is this alive after dark, and I for one approve of all of this gamboling about. Suzanne, this festival matches my preferred hours perfectly, though probably not yours," Grace said as she looked around at the half-full racks of donuts left, Band Busters and all. "How's business, or do I even need to ask?"

"Not wonderful, but then again, it's not during my normal operating hours, so it's not an issue. We're raising some money for the band, so I can't complain."

"Are you donating all of the supplies to the cause yourself?" she asked me critically. Grace knew what a thin profit margin I ran on at Donut Hearts, and she was always looking out for me financially. She was a savvy businesswoman, something that I found too easy to forget sometimes because of the easygoing way she treated her job.

"I am, but don't worry about me. I can handle the hit," I said, not willing to admit that my donation of raw materials, even discounting my time and Emma's salary for the extra working hours, would eat a deep hole in that month's profits.

"Tell you what. Let *me* cover them for you," Grace said softly. "Things have been very good at work lately. We blew past our sales goals this quarter, and everyone, including the supervisors, just got a nice bonus."

Grace worked for a cosmetics company as a regional supervisor, and from everything I could see, she did well at it, though she generally worked quite a few hours less than I did. I would have loved to hit the minimum wage mark myself. In truth, I was exaggerating, but not by much.

"Thanks for the offer, but I've got it. There's no reason for you to spend your hard-earned money on me or my donut shop."

"Suzanne, there's no reason to be a hero. Besides, I wasn't talking about dipping into my own personal bank account. I have a budget for PR that I have to use up in the next few days or I'll lose it. What better cause can you think of than this?"

"Honestly, you should use it for something else," I said, determined to do it on my own. I was reluctant to accept her offer, even though it would help me a great deal. It was probably just stubborn pride.

Grace just shrugged. "Suit yourself, but I have to spend it all somewhere, or I won't get as much next quarter."

"For the life of me, I don't understand the corporate world sometimes," I said.

"It's not the easiest thing in the world to do, but it has its perks," she said. "Are you sure you don't want the donation? Honestly, you'd be helping me out if you took it."

Leave it to Grace to couch her generosity as a favor request. I struggled with the idea of accepting her donation for another moment or two before I spoke again. "If I took your money, how could we advertise your participation in the program? Spirit Night is already halfway over."

"That's not an issue," she said with a smile as she handed me a check. The sneaky rascal had already made it out before she'd even stepped one foot inside my donut shop.

"This is way too much, Grace," I replied as I tried to hand it back to her.

"Then donate what's left after your expenses to the uniform fund. There's just one catch, though."

"What's that?"

Grace frowned, and then she asked me, "Would you mind putting a sign in your window that my company participated in the event by sponsoring you? I just need to take a picture of it and send it in to Corporate, and you can pull the sign down as soon as I have my photo."

I thought about it for a moment, and then I countered her suggestion with one of my own. "I can do better than that. Make a banner and I'll put it up in the front window for a week," I said.

"Are you sure you wouldn't mind? That would be perfect. I'll be back in fifteen minutes," Grace said, and then she handed me her pennant. "In the meantime, wave this around every now and then. Go Dogs."

I had to laugh as my best friend hurried back out into the crowd, narrowly avoiding being run over by two ghosts, one leaning heavily on the other. Evidently someone had gotten more into the spirits than the actual spirit of the event. Leave it to Grace to step in and save the day. I had to admit that having that check made me breathe a lot easier. Maybe now

I could actually enjoy the sleep deprivation I'd be undergoing soon. I decided to be a little more active, so I grabbed a nice selection of donuts and put them on a tray, focusing mainly on the blue and gold donuts I'd made for the event, as well as the spirit ghost ones. I couldn't exactly wander around the park, leave the donut shop unattended, and risk something happening while I was gone, but there was no reason I couldn't sit out front at one of the Donut Hearts tables and peddle my goods from a spot closer to the action.

From my new perspective, I had a bird's-eye view of the park across the street where the majority of the festivities were taking place. The school band was set up in the gazebo, and a dozen vendors, all donating their proceeds to the cause, were tightly wedged around it. A bonfire ready and waiting to be lit had been built close to the Boxcar Grill, and I realized that I'd have had a wonderful view of it from the porch of my cottage. For a moment I wished that Jake were there to take all of it in with me, but he was on the North Carolina coast dealing with the murder of the mayor of a beach resort. It was a real puzzler, the only type of case that Jake seemed to get. That was a real hitch with being so good at what he did, and his boss was squeezing every last drop of work out of him before he was gone for good.

I enjoyed the excitement as folks of all ages paraded past the shop, laughing at the ghosts as they wandered in and out of the festivities, and I even managed to sell a few donuts as time went by, too. I loved this time of year. The days were growing shorter and the evenings chillier, and this evening was no exception. Soon the bonfire would be lit, and folks would enjoy the dancing flames long into the night, sipping their hot cocoa—and other drinks—and reveling in their friendships.

When all was said and done, it would be a time to remember, a slice of the small town life that I loved so dearly.

I decided that as soon as they lit the bonfire, I'd close

Donut Hearts and join everyone else.

"Hey, you haven't closed the shop yet, have you?" Grace asked as she hurried to me with the promised banner in her hands.

"No, of course not. Is that it?"

She grinned. "It turned out to be a little bigger than I'd originally planned. To tell you the truth, I got a little carried away. I'll let you off the hook. You just have to leave it up long enough for me to take a few photos of it."

"Nonsense. I meant what I said. I'm going to leave it up all week so folks know that you and your company played a part in my donation," I said. We walked back into the shop and draped her signage across the window, a sweet banner she'd printed out on her computer that looked extremely professional. "That's great. I might have you do some advertisements for the shop if I ever scrape up enough to cover the expense."

"I'd be happy to do it," Grace said with a smile. There was no denying that she was a lovely woman, stylish and fit, but in my opinion, it was her smile that made her so beautiful. My best friend had an easy way with people that proved she had been born for sales, and she took full advantage of it. When we were finished hanging the new banner, we both took a step back and admired her handiwork. "Wow, that turned out even better than I hoped it would." After taking several photos with her camera, she asked, "Are you sure you want to leave this up? It's kind of big."

"So was your generous donation," I said. "How long do you think I should stay open tonight?"

"I don't know. You have quite a few donuts left," Grace said as she studied the display shelves.

"True, but I don't have to sell them all now that you've contributed so generously to the cause. Why don't we give them out to the crowd, courtesy of your company and Donut Hearts? What do you think of that idea?"

"I think it's brilliant. Plus, it sounds like a lot of fun. Let's do it."

We gathered the remaining donuts onto one cart I used sometimes for street fairs and other events, and I locked Donut Hearts behind me, leaving the lights on so folks could see Grace's banner even though we were closed. I knew that she'd made the donation to help me, but I wanted to give her a good return for her kind investment.

We were just getting started giving out donuts to a crowd of grateful attendees when I heard the first scream.

Even though I'd never heard her scream before, I knew in an instant who it had to be.

Something had clearly provoked Emma Blake so strongly that it had made her cry out into the night, a shriek that rose above all of the background noise of the festivities, and I was determined to find out what exactly had happened to make her shriek like that.

Chapter 3

"He's dead!" Emma shouted through her sobs as she gestured wildly toward the freshly lit bonfire.

"Who's dead, Emma?" I asked as I tried to calm her down while searching for what she'd seen.

"Him! Can't you see him?" She stood there in shock, pointing to the heart of the fire, which was freshly lit and starting to lick its way up the piled wooden branches and planks.

I looked harder, and sure enough, I saw what looked like a man's body hidden within the wood, newly illuminated by the growing tongues of fire. I couldn't tell whether he was dead or alive, but I knew that I had to act quickly before it was too late. "Somebody help me!" I yelled as I abandoned my donut cart and started running toward the flames. I'd had a bad experience with fire in the not-so-distant past, but that didn't keep me from doing what I knew that I had to do.

The fire chief had lit the bonfire himself, and he hurried to cut me off me as I rushed toward the growing flames.

"Suzanne, what's wrong?" he asked me. "What do you think you're doing?"

"There! Look!" In my excitement, I seemed to have lost my ability to utter more than one word at a time.

The fire chief took in the scene and quickly spotted the body. In his defense, he most likely couldn't have seen it from the ignition point where he'd first lit the fire. It was a credit to his training and skills that he didn't even hesitate once he saw what was going on. Because the fire had been built close to the diner—not to mention my cottage—the fire department was already there in case of emergency, and this certainly qualified as one. In a matter of moments, under his direction, the chief's entire crew leapt into action, going from collecting donations in rubber boots into full-fledged firefighting mode. The hose was manned and the flames were out quickly before any damage could be done to the body.

I watched as the fire chief started to move closer toward the woodpile when I saw a firm hand come out of the crowd and grab his shoulder. It was Chief Martin, my freshly minted stepfather, and temporarily back on the job as chief of police.

"You need to stand down. I'll take it from here," Chief Martin said with the calm voice of authority, and the fire chief nodded in quick agreement. He might have even looked a little relieved in the light coming from the streetlamp nearby. Well, why wouldn't he be happy to let the police handle the situation? He'd been trained to put out fires, not investigate homicides. Though he had probably seen his share of dead bodies over the years, I imagined that those deaths had been caused by fire, not occurring before the fires had even started. It was an entirely different type of investigation, and one that our chief of police had plenty of experience with.

For that matter, so had I.

"Is that Rick Hastings?" I asked the chief as I got closer to the body.

"Suzanne, you need to step away. I don't have time to answer any of your questions right now; I need to handle this."

"Sure. I understand," I said as I stepped back and let him do what he had to do. I knew that it was hard enough on the chief to come back to a job he clearly didn't want, and I didn't want to make things even more difficult for him if I didn't have to.

It appeared that murder had once again come to pay a visit to April Springs.

But who was the victim, and why had someone decided to leave the body in such a conspicuous place? Was it indeed Rick Hastings, Emma's boyfriend, or was it some other unfortunate soul? From where I stood, I had no idea, and I was glad that it wasn't my job to figure it out.

In the end, I was a donutmaker, by vocation as well as avocation, and I planned on sticking with what I did best and let the police handle this on their own.

That was my initial intention, at any rate, and it continued to be so right up until the second I learned exactly who the victim was, and how the murder would directly affect my life.

Chapter 4

"Did you see who it was?" Grace asked me softly as she and Emma joined me near the dampened bonfire, a spot that was now clearly a crime scene.

"I can't tell for sure, and the police chief's not saying," I said, doing my best to keep my voice calm and level. Emma was already on the edge, and she didn't need any signs that her worst fears might be true.

"It's Rick. I just know it is," Emma said, her voice completely deadened with pain. Even as she spoke, she couldn't seem to pull her gaze away from the body as the chief and his deputies photographed and videotaped the details of the crime scene for their records.

"We don't know that for sure yet," I said as I put an arm around my assistant and good friend and did my best to comfort her.

"You may not know, Suzanne, but I do," she said.

"Emma? Are you all right?" Sharon Blake, Emma's mother, asked as she rushed toward us.

"Oh, Mom. It's just awful." Emma wrapped her arms around her mother and held on for dear life. I watched as Sharon stroked her daughter's hair, and was glad that she'd found her in the crowd.

"It's going to be okay," Sharon said so softly that I almost missed it.

"How can it be? I just know that it's Rick," Emma choked out.

"If it is, then we'll all find a way to get through it together," Sharon said, her voice full of calm reassurance.

That seemed to pacify Emma a little, but I noticed that neither mother nor daughter made any move to break their embrace. After a few more moments, Sharon asked me softly, "Suzanne, would you ask the police chief if he's been able to make a positive identification yet?"

"I'll try, but I can't make any promises that I'll get an

answer," I said.

"Just do your best," Sharon said, and then she turned her full attention back to her daughter.

As I left them both and hurried toward Chief Martin, I noticed that Grace was right on my heels.

"He's not going to tell us anything. You know that, don't you?" Grace asked me gently once we were away from the mother and daughter.

"You're probably right, but I have to at least try. You heard her."

"I'm not saying that you shouldn't ask Chief Martin. Just don't expect to get any answers," Grace said. "I've got a thought. If the chief won't tell us anything, which has turned out to be the case so far, maybe I can get something out of Stephen." The Stephen she was referring to was Stephen Grant, an officer on the April Springs police force, and more importantly to Grace, her current boyfriend.

"Just try not to get him into any more trouble with his boss," I said. I knew that Officer Grant was often in hot water with the police chief, and he didn't need our help getting in any deeper than he normally was.

"I'll try not to, but I'm not making any promises, either," Grace said as she went off in search of her boyfriend.

I just shrugged as I started angling back toward the police chief. Odds were that he wasn't going to tell me anything after dismissing me earlier, but I'd told Sharon that I'd try, so that was exactly what I was going to do.

"Chief, I know that you're busy, but do you have one second? I wouldn't ask you if it weren't important," I said as he finished directing two of his deputies as they unfurled their crime scene tape, enclosing a large chunk of the park as they unwound it from its spool.

"Sorry, Suzanne. Honestly, right now I don't have a single second to spare."

"Even if it's just one question?" I persisted.

The chief looked at me with that same exasperated expression I'd grown used to over the years, but then he must have remembered that he couldn't so easily discount me as he once had now that we were family, related through both of our relationships with my mother. "Make it quick. What's your question?" he asked, failing to hide his impatience with being interrupted during his investigation.

"Is the body Rick Hastings'?" I asked.

The chief's gaze grew suddenly suspicious. "What makes you say that? I know for a fact that there's no way you could have seen who it was in the dark."

I felt my heart freeze a little with the confirmation. "Does that mean that it's true, then?"

In a lower voice, Chief Martin answered, "It is, but I still want to know how you knew it was him."

"Emma told me," I admitted.

"And how exactly did she know?"

"Chief, she's been dating Rick for a month," I explained. "She had to have known him better than either one of us could have."

"That doesn't explain how she could have spotted him in that bonfire just as it was being lit. I was standing nearby myself, and I could barely make out that it was a man at all, let alone identify the body."

"I don't know what to tell you; I can't explain it. She must have seen *something* that told her that it was him," I said, completely skirting the idea that it might have been her woman's intuition. Chief Martin wasn't a big fan of the expression, and I wasn't about to use it after he'd just given me valuable information.

I was about to ask him if he knew yet how Rick had died when I felt a nudge behind me. I turned, fully expecting to find Grace, but instead, Ray Blake was crowding me. He was Emma's father, and he owned and operated our local newspaper, *The April Springs Sentinel*. It was more a delivery vehicle for coupons and ads than it was a newsbreaking machine, but that never discouraged Ray from trying to scoop everyone at the larger papers that were based nearby.

"Who was the victim, Chief?" Ray asked him.

"No comment," the chief said, clearly with practiced ease.

The newspaperman looked aggravated. "Seriously? I know for a fact that you were just talking to Suzanne a second ago, and I can't imagine you brushing her off now that she's your stepdaughter. If she knows something, the entire citizenry of April Springs has a right to know it, too."

"Like I said, no comment," the chief repeated. At that moment, he reminded me a little of Jake. I hadn't always been the police chief's biggest fan, but since I'd started working around the edges of law enforcement on a few homicide cases myself, I'd developed a little more respect for the man's skills. His job was hard, there was no doubt about it, and I couldn't imagine how he managed to do it as well as he did.

Ray wasn't about to be discouraged by the flat refusal, though. Instead of focusing on the chief, he turned to me instead. "Suzanne, who was the victim? Do I need to remind you that you're not under any obligation to keep secrets for the police department?"

"Ray, how's Emma doing?" I asked pointedly as I ignored his question.

He dismissed my question with an irritable shrug. "I'm sure she's fine. How is that pertinent to this situation?"

"Didn't you know? She's the one who first saw the body, and she was pretty traumatized by the discovery when I saw her. Don't you think that you should check on her? Your daughter might need you."

That got his attention. Suddenly the newsman in front of me was replaced by the caring father. "Where is she?"

"The last time I saw her, she was somewhere over that way," I said as I pointed in the general direction where I'd seen Emma and her mother last. I decided to share that information with him as well. "She was with Sharon the last time I saw her, but she was still falling apart. I've got a feeling that she needs both of you right now."

Ray took off into the crowd without another word, and the

man earned a point or two with me by doing so, abandoning the possibility of a hot story so that he could look after his daughter's welfare.

"Thanks for that," the chief said after Ray was gone.

"You might not be thanking me in a minute when I tell you what I'm probably going to have to do," I told him.

Chief Martin shook his head for a moment before he spoke. When he finally did talk again, there was more resignation in his voice than disapproval. "Let me guess. You and Grace are going to dig into this murder yourselves, aren't you?"

I smiled at him. "You got it on the first guess. I really don't have any choice, Chief. Emma is like family to me."

"I'm perfectly aware of that fact," he said with a sigh. "Just try not to muddy the investigation too much, will you?"

"I'll do my best," I said, happy that he really did see some value in what Grace and I did.

"Keep me posted, and I mean about everything you uncover. Oh, and one more thing. Stay safe. Your mother would kill me if I let something happen to you."

"You know me. I'm *always* careful," I said with another smile, and then, completely on impulse, I kissed his cheek. "Thanks."

"You're welcome," he said, clearly embarrassed by the brief display of affection. "Just don't make me regret it, okay?"

"Yes, sir," I said. "Now, could you tell me exactly how the man was murdered?"

He grinned at me before he spoke. "I'll tell you exactly what I just told Ray Blake."

"No comment?" I asked, returning his smile in kind.

"Hey, you're good at this game, too. Now do me a favor and scram. I've got work to do."

"I'm already gone," I said. "Oh, just one last thing."

"What is it, Suzanne? Don't press your luck too far."

"I just realized that somebody needs to tell Emma Blake. She's been dating Rick for the past month, so she has a right to know before it becomes common knowledge, don't you think?"

"You're right, of course. I absolutely hate that part of my job," Chief Martin said sadly, and I could see that he meant it. It had to be awful informing loved ones that someone they cared about would never be coming back to them again, and I didn't envy him the task one little bit.

"Would you like me to tell her for you?" I volunteered.

After a moment of hesitation, the police chief shook his head. "No. Thanks for the offer, but I'll do it."

"Are you sure?"

"It's my job, Suzanne, but I appreciate the gesture. As a matter of fact, I'd better go take care of that right now."

I nodded, and then I watched the man walk away. All in all, it was probably a good thing that he'd refused my offer. A part of me had wanted to speak with Emma about her boyfriend so I could get some leads that might help Grace and me find his killer, but mostly I knew in my heart that there was no way that I could bring myself to ask those hard questions, at least not yet. Right now I needed for her to find out that her worst fears had been realized, and then I had to give her some time and space to cope with the knowledge before I questioned her. After all, my friend's state of mind counted for a great deal more than any murder investigation. I'd offer her comfort if I could, but I wouldn't bring up Rick's name until I felt she was ready to deal with what had happened to him.

Until that occurred, Grace and I were going to have to conduct our investigation without her, because there was no way that I was going to add to Emma's pain if I could help it.

Where was Grace, anyway? She should have been back by now. I grabbed my phone and started to punch in her number when I saw her walking toward me in the muted light coming from the lamps scattered around the park.

"I was just getting ready to call you. Where have you been?" I asked her.

"Searching in vain for my boyfriend," she answered. "I hope you had better luck than I did."

Lowering my voice, I said, "It's not public knowledge yet, but Chief Martin confirmed that Emma was right. It was Rick Hastings' body."

Grace looked at me in awe. "How did you get him to admit that to you?"

"I'm not sure. I must have caught him at a weak moment," I said.

"Did you get anything else?"

"No, that's all that he would tell me," I replied.

"Poor Emma. Who's going to tell her?"

"I volunteered, but the chief said that it was part of his job. I'll say this for the man; he takes his responsibilities seriously. I don't think I would have the heart for it."

"I don't have the stomach, either," Grace said. "So, where does that leave us?"

I looked around and saw that most of the crowd of onlookers had dispersed. The body had just been removed from the bonfire, and all that remained on the scene was the police tape marking off the area as a crew of officers scoured the surrounding area using flashlights to brighten the weak illumination. If there was a clue to be found anywhere in the trampled grass, I hoped that they found it. Grace and I wouldn't be any help in the search, and honestly, we'd probably just get in the way even if we tried to join in.

"I'm not sure that there's anything we can do right now," I said. "I say we get together tomorrow after the donut shop closes and see what we can learn about Rick Hastings on our own. Do you think you can get away from work a little early?"

"I don't see why not," she said with a smile. "Sometimes I just love being the boss." Grace hesitated a moment, and then she added, "Frankly, I'm kind of surprised that you're opening Donut Hearts tomorrow at all. You realize that you can't count on Emma to come in, don't you?" After another moment, she added, "I could always take a sick day and help out if you're that desperate."

I knew what a sacrifice it would be for my best friend to get up so early, so I appreciated the gesture more than I could express. "No worries. I can manage just fine on my own. Don't forget, I run the shop one day a week by myself on Emma's day off, so I can certainly handle the shop tomorrow solo."

"What if she doesn't make it back the next day, either?"

"Grace, I can go it alone as long as I need to," I said. "Obviously I'd rather have Emma with me, but until she feels ready to get back to work, I'm going to do it all myself."

"Suzanne, you're a good employer, but you're an even better friend," Grace said as we started to walk through the park toward the cottage where I lived.

"Well, I try to be," I said as we neared my front porch. "Would you like to come in for a few minutes before you head down the road?"

Grace shook her head. "Thanks for the invitation, but you need your sleep. I'll see you tomorrow morning at eleven thirty."

"That sounds great. Good night."

"Night," she replied as she headed down the road, taking the three dozen steps to her own home. It had been wonderful having my best friend living so close when we'd been growing up, but I loved it even more now. Apart from my time being married to Max, I'd lived at the cottage all of my life, and up until fairly recently, I'd been there with my mother. Nothing lasts forever, though, and she'd moved across town to start over when she'd married the police chief, so now I lived on my own.

I probably should have eaten something healthy when I got home, but I was exhausted, both from the murder and from doing another session of donutmaking in the evening. Instead of preparing something nutritious, I ended up grabbing a quick bite of the apple pie that Momma had brought over the day before that was now in my fridge, and as I was pouring a glass of milk to go with it, my cellphone rang.

"Hey, Jake," I said as my weariness suddenly vanished, happy to know that my fiancé had been thinking about me and had been able to get away long enough to call. "How are things going on the coast?"

"It's complicated," Jake said, and I could hear the exhaustion in his voice.

"I still can't believe that your boss is making you work your full notice," I said. "I wish that you were here."

"I do, too, but I don't have that much time left. It will be over before we know it. Besides, I gave my word when I took this job that I'd work a fair notice, and I mean to do just that. To be honest with you, I was kind of surprised that he wanted me to stay, but since he does, I'm going to stick it out until the bitter end. This is important to me."

"I know that," I said, "and that's one of the things that I admire most about you. I just wish that you didn't have to be so far away."

"Me, too. Now, tell me about your day. I trust that Spirit Night turned out better for you than my night did for me."

"I wish I could tell you that it did, but unfortunately something happened."

"Are you okay, Suzanne?" he asked me, sudden concern coming through in his voice.

"I'm fine, and so is everyone else I love," I answered. "Emma's boyfriend was murdered tonight, though."

"That's terrible," Jake said. "What happened?"

"At this point we're still waiting to hear."

"Are you saying that you know that he was murdered, but you don't know how? Explain that to me."

I took a deep breath, let it out slowly, and then I said, "His body was propped onto the bonfire in the park, and nobody even noticed that he was there until the fire chief lit the fire and Emma spotted the figure in the growing flames."

"Man, that couldn't have been easy on her." After a brief pause, he asked, "How does someone ditch a body in a pile of wood in the middle of the evening when the whole town is out and about? It's kind of conspicuous, isn't it?"

"I haven't figured that out yet, and I've been wondering about that myself. It didn't help that half the crowd was dressed up as ghosts or wearing other costumes, and the other half was sporting blue and gold everything. It makes me wonder just how long he was there before Emma spotted him," I said. It was an intriguing question. Had Rick been there long, or was his positioning on the bonfire mere happenstance? There were some very good reasons to think that he'd been murdered on the spot. After all, there was no way the killer could drag the body very far without being discovered; Rick was a pretty big guy. Did that mean that there was a bullet hole, or maybe even a stab wound that no one had found yet? It wasn't even out of the realm of possibility that he could have been poisoned and had fallen into the fire's wooden stockpile himself when the toxin finally struck home. I knew that we'd find out sooner or later, but I wanted to know now.

"Suzanne? Are you still there?" Jake asked, bringing me back to the present.

"Sorry. I was just thinking about something."

"That makes sense. I thought I could hear the gears turning from here," he said with a dull laugh.

"It's just frustrating how much I don't know."

"Well, at least you know the victim's identity."

"That's it, though, Jake. I have a ton of other theories about what might have happened to him, but there's nothing that I can confirm."

"Is there anything in particular that you'd like to run past me? Who knows? I might even be able to help."

I considered telling him about the possibilities I'd been contemplating, but then I realized that this man had enough on his mind without me adding to it. "Thanks for the offer, but there's nothing just yet."

"Well, keep me posted." There was a moment's pause as someone away from the phone spoke to him, and he returned to me as he said, "Sorry. I've got to go."

It was so abrupt that I didn't get a chance to say good night, or that I loved him, or repeat that I wished he was in April Springs with me, but I was used to it. When Jake was on a case, he had unbelievable focus, and anything personal got left on the periphery.

I should be able to recognize it, since lately I'd become the same way myself when I was investigating a murder.

Maybe it was an occupational hazard of the job, and I had it, even though for me, this was still a hobby; a deadly serious hobby, but a hobby nonetheless.

I started to head for the master bedroom downstairs where I slept these days, but for some reason, I found myself climbing the steps to my old room instead. I changed into a spare set of jammies I kept up there, and then I settled in for the night in my old familiar spot. From the window near the bed I could see part of the park clearly outside, though I couldn't make out the outline of the unburned bonfire anymore. Still, the second-story view of the familiar surroundings gave me comfort on a night where it was in short supply, so I curled up into my bed and found myself falling asleep before I knew what was happening.

Tomorrow would come soon enough, so I embraced the slumber, knowing that I'd get precious little rest before it was time to get up again.

Chapter 5

"Sharon, what are you doing here?" I asked Emma's mother the next morning after I answered the knocking on the back door of the donut shop an hour after I'd arrived. "I thought you'd be home with your daughter, or at the very least, still asleep."

"Honestly, that was my original plan, but Emma wouldn't go to sleep last night until I promised I'd come by and offer you my assistance this morning," the older woman said as she smiled at me. "If you don't want me here, just say the word and I'll be on my way, but I promised Emma that I would at least try."

"How is she doing?"

"I'm worried about her, if you want to know the truth," Sharon said gravely.

"Is she falling apart?" I asked, envisioning all sorts of meltdowns. It had to be tough losing someone so close. Even if Rick hadn't been the perfect boyfriend, they had been in a relationship, and she'd lost him.

"It's just the opposite," Sharon said. "Emma keeps insisting that she's fine, but I know better. If anything, she's in complete denial, but I don't know how long that will last before the reality of what happened starts to sink in."

"We both know that Emma is tough deep down where it counts. She'll find her way through this if anyone can," I said.

"I hope you're right. So, do I take off my jacket, or do I go back home?"

I suddenly realized that I was pretty far behind in my morning chores. Emma and I hadn't finished cleaning up the night before, given all that had happened, and I hadn't spent much time yet that morning washing dishes. In fact, I'd added to the mess by making the cake donuts first, working around the dirty pots and pans in the sink and on the counter in back. I was planning to get to them later, but I wasn't exactly sure when that would be.

"That depends. Do you honestly mean your offer to help, or are you just following your daughter's wishes?" I asked her with a grin.

"Go on. Put me to work," she said with a smile. "I'm sure that you must have a mound of dishes that you haven't had time to deal with yet, especially since you were open last night."

"I'll be honest with you; it's a train wreck back there," I admitted. "I'd love to have you, and I'm more than happy to put you on the payroll, but only if you're sure you don't mind."

"Suzanne, I'll do whatever you need me to do, but I won't take a dime for any of it," Sharon said.

"Then we have a problem, because I can't let you work for free," I said with a frown.

"Well, it's not exactly free," she said with the hint of a grin. "What I'd really like you to do is to pay Emma instead of me."

"I appreciate the gesture, but that's nonsense. She'll get her standard pay, and so will you." It would mean cutting things a little closer to the bone than I usually liked for the next several days, but that didn't matter to me at the moment. Besides, Grace had taken care of my current shortfall I'd incurred from my donation the night before, so why not use my profits the way I liked?

It was Sharon's turn to smile at my gesture. "Suzanne, don't kid yourself; we both know how thin your profit margin is around here. I won't have you losing money because of the Blake girls."

"You let me worry about that," I said. "I had a healthy donation last night that's fattened my bottom line unexpectedly, and I can't think of a better use for it than this. Now, if you're sure that you don't mind, I'd greatly appreciate it if you'd take off your coat, grab an apron, and dive in. I need to ice the cake donuts and get the yeast dough ready for proofing."

"Trust me, I know the routine," Sharon said as she walked into the back with me.

By the time we were ready for our first break, the kitchen was immaculate again, and everything was in its place. "Do you and Emma go outside for your breaks when you're running Donut Hearts for me?" I asked Sharon as I set the portable timer that told me when the dough would be ready for its next step.

"You bet we do, rain or shine, hot or cold," Sharon replied. "Emma insisted that we do it that way from the very start, and to be honest with you, I've really grown to enjoy it."

"Then let's bundle up and head outside," I said as I grabbed the timer so we'd know when our break was over and the dough would be ready for its next phase.

I zipped up my jacket as we walked outside of the donut shop and into the darkness. It was getting chillier with the passing of each day and night, and I wondered how soon the snow might start flying. April Springs got a smattering of the white stuff every year, usually two or three snowfalls annually that were mostly melted by noon, but every now and then we got hammered with the mother of all snowstorms, and the entire town shut down when that happened.

To be more exact, everyone but the town maintenance crew that ran the snowplows, and my donut shop. I always trudged through the snow in the steady gray night and made my donuts regardless of the weather. After all, the men and women who kept our streets clear deserved a treat, and so did any brave and intrepid soul willing to venture out into the winter wonderland.

As Sharon and I settled in at the table in front of Donut Hearts where our breaks always took place, she surprised me by saying exactly what I'd just been thinking. "I hope we get lots and lots of snow this year," Sharon said after she took a deep sip of warm coffee. "The almanac says that we're due."

"I was just thinking the same thing," I admitted. "I've got

all of my supplies laid in, so I'm ready, if and when it happens."

"Do you mean at the cottage?" Sharon asked me.

"No, though I have food and firewood aplenty there as well. I'm talking about the donut shop. We never seem to lose power here, so if I have electricity to run things, I can always make donuts."

"I remember the time George borrowed someone's snowmobile and came by to collect you and Emma during a particularly heavy snowfall. My daughter still tells that story to this day."

I recalled it as well, back before the mayor had become the mayor and was just a retired cop who helped me occasionally with my investigations. Momma hadn't been married then, but at least I'd known Jake. Sometimes it was hard to remember a time when he wasn't in my life. "It was quite a ride," I said. "You know, I probably don't say it enough, but it's truly wonderful having your daughter here."

"Suzanne, she loves this donut shop nearly as much as you do," Sharon said. "I can't tell you how much Ray and I appreciate you making room for her."

"She's my most valuable asset. As long as I'm running Donut Hearts, she'll be here if she wants to be. Truthfully, I can't imagine running the place without her," I said, and then added hastily, "not that I don't appreciate all that you're doing, as well."

"Oh, I know that I'm capable enough, but I can't match my daughter's skills, and honestly, I'm fine with that. Her offerings of coffees alone set her apart from anything that I would ever even dream of attempting."

"Emma does have a flair for the unusual," I said. I glanced at the timer and saw that we had a few more minutes left on our break. I was wondering if I should ask Sharon about Emma's boyfriend, or if I should just leave it alone, when she made the decision for me.

"Suzanne, Emma wanted me to ask you something, but if I'm overstepping my bounds, please let me know. No hard feelings."

"Go on. Your daughter and I usually have a pretty open dialogue that covers just about everything, so I'll extend the same privilege to you if you'd like."

"I'd greatly appreciate that." Sharon took a deep breath, and then she said, "Emma wants to know if you'll investigate Rick's murder. If you haven't already decided to look into it, she asked me to implore you and Grace to find out what really happened to him."

"We're already digging around some," I admitted, "but we don't want to make things any worse for Emma than they already are, so we're reluctant to speak with her about him until she's ready."

"As you said earlier, my daughter is tougher than she looks. She knows that Chief Martin is good at what he does, but she also believes that you manage to get to the heart of matters that aren't as readily apparent to others. For what it's worth, I think so myself. We'd both consider it an enormous favor if you'd do it."

"First of all, it's important that you remember that I never do anything alone. Even *with* a great deal of help from others, more times than not it boils down to Grace and me simply getting lucky."

"Do you know my definition of luck, Suzanne?" she asked with a wry smile.

I certainly should, since Emma had shared it with me enough times over the years. "Luck is nothing more than when preparation meets opportunity," I said.

Sharon laughed out loud when she heard my quote. "I see that my daughter has been talking about me."

"Only good things," I answered.

"I'm not naïve enough to believe that," Sharon said, "but thanks for the effort. Most of the time, my daughter and I get along splendidly. Working side by side here with her when you've been gone has been a real blessing. It's brought us even closer together, and I'm indebted to you for every opportunity that we've had. As a matter of fact, most of the times we've clashed in the last five years have been over the boys and men that she's dated."

"Does that include Rick Hastings?" I asked.

"Especially Rick," Sharon replied gravely. "I know that it's not generally acceptable to speak ill of the dead, but I never liked that man, not from the first moment he crossed my threshold."

"What in particular didn't you like about him?"

Sharon sighed, and then she said, "Let me count the ways. In the first place, he was too old for her. In the second, he had no visible means of support, and yet he always seemed to have plenty of money to throw around. Finally, I didn't care for the company he kept when he wasn't around Emma."

"Was there anyone in particular you had a problem with?" I asked, hoping that Sharon might be able to shed some light as to where Grace and I should start our investigation.

"If I had the time, I could make you a list," Sharon said, clearly being sarcastic about her suggestion.

"Would you? That would be great," I said as the timer went off.

"Sure, I don't see why not. Do we need to go back in now? I could give you a brief rundown right now," Sharon volunteered.

We had chores to do inside, but I wasn't ready to postpone my investigation quite just yet. "We can probably push it a few minutes," I reassured her.

"Nonsense. Let's go in. You see about the yeast donuts and I'll think about my list as I tackle more tasks inside. By opening, I'll have something ready for you. How does that sound?"

"Perfect," I said, though I really wanted to hear her thoughts immediately. Not that it mattered. I couldn't do anything about whatever she told me until Donut Hearts was closed for the day and I was free to start sleuthing with Grace, so I was just going to have to take what I could get.

As I worked on taking the yeast donut dough through its

various stages, I found myself wondering who exactly would make it onto Sharon's list, but I couldn't come up with a single name, even though it shouldn't have been a real surprise to me. Sharon had enjoyed more proximity and a deeper relationship with her daughter than the two of us could ever have, and after all, that was as it should have been. Even though Emma and I worked together, she usually didn't talk about her current boyfriends, especially when she knew that I didn't approve of them. I hadn't said anything overtly disparaging about Rick, but it probably hadn't been that difficult for Emma to pick up on my true feelings.

After all, I'd never been very good at concealing them.

We were loading the day's offerings into the display cases up front just before we were set to open when Sharon handed me a folded sheet of paper.

"These four names were all that I was able to come up with," she explained.

"You managed to list that many people?" I asked her, incredulous.

"What can I say? Emma tells me just about everything going on in her life, and I'm a very good listener. These names might not have represented red flags to her, but I was concerned enough to note them all when she told me about them."

I opened the paper and studied the names written there. I was surprised to find that I knew two of them fairly well, and I had a passing acquaintance with a third. Only the last name written was unfamiliar to me, though I knew that wouldn't last for long. Once Grace and I started digging into the lives of our potential murderers, I was sure that we'd soon know a great deal more about the folks on Sharon's list.

There were three men and one woman written down on that piece of paper: Travis Wright, Kyle Creasy, Denny West, and Amanda Moore. I knew that Travis owned a small construction company, while Kyle was a landscaper. They both came into the donut shop every now and then, separately of course. I didn't know what Amanda Moore did for a living, but she had been in Donut Hearts only once that I could recall, while Denny West was a complete stranger to me.

"Thanks for doing this," I said as I tucked the note into my front jeans pocket.

"Do you think it will be of any help to you?" Sharon asked me as I headed for the front door to unlock it and open the donut shop for business. "I don't really know why any of them had a problem with Rick, just that they did."

"It's too soon to tell where things stand right now, but at least you've given us someplace to start."

"Just be careful," Sharon said before I got to the door.

I looked outside, but no one was waiting to get in. "Why, did you just see something outside?"

"That's not what I meant. I'm talking about the people on the list I gave you who were associated with Rick Hastings. I have a hunch that there was a good reason that he came to a bad end."

"I promise you that Grace and I will both watch our steps," I said. Unlocking the door, I stepped outside for a moment to take in the early morning air. The day hadn't had a chance to warm up yet, and there was definitely still some of that chill in the air that we'd enjoyed earlier. I could even smell wood smoke as I took a deep breath, a sure sign that cold weather was indeed on its way.

It was a full fifteen minutes before anyone came into the shop, and I was wondering what was keeping my regulars away. Summer was usually our dreariest season, but every now and then, for no obvious reason, we had a lull in business even as cold weather approached. I'd tried my best to understand it, hoping that I could learn to explain the hiatus, but I'd never come up with a good solution except that everybody in town suddenly decided that they'd had their fill of donuts for the time being. The sales drought usually only lasted a couple of days, but once it had approached two weeks, and I'd started to panic at the thought of closing Donut Hearts down forever and getting a real job. I worked hard at my shop, no one could deny it, but it was work that I loved.

Finally, our first customer of the day showed up, but it wasn't some random resident of April Springs.

It was our mayor, George Morris.

"Hey there, Your Honor," I greeted George as he walked in the door.

"Hello there, yourself. I wasn't sure that you'd be open, what with what happened to Emma's new boyfriend last night. The scuttlebutt around town is that you'll be closed until further notice until she has a chance to deal with her grief."

At least that explained our lack of customers. "No, we're open today, tomorrow, and the day after, same as always."

"Are you here all by yourself?" the mayor asked as he looked around the shop. The question might have been creepy coming from anyone else, but I trusted George with my life, and I'd proved it in the past on more than one occasion.

"No, Sharon's helping me out in back," I said. "What can I get you this morning?"

He studied the display case intently, and then after a moment, he said, "Tell you what; why don't you pick."

I grabbed one of his favorites, a simple cake donut, and poured him a plain coffee, black. "Here you go. You're a man of simple tastes; you know that, don't you?"

George winked at me as he took a bite of donut, and then he followed it up with a sip of coffee. "Suzanne, you know me too well."

"How's Polly doing?" I asked him. His girlfriend—and his secretary at the town hall—had been away a great deal lately watching over her grandchildren, and I knew that George missed her a lot, though he was reluctant to admit it to anyone, even me.

"As a matter of fact, she's coming back to town this very

afternoon," George said with a smile, and then he took another bite of his donut.

"So, is that why you're eating donuts while you still can?" I asked him with a grin. Polly had him on a fairly strict diet, one that didn't include my tasty treats, but while she was away, George took it as a sign that he could eat whatever he wanted to.

"I figure that what she doesn't know can't hurt her," he answered. "Suzanne, you're not going to tell on me, are you?"

"You should know better than that. I consider anything that goes on between me and my customers as privileged information," I replied with another smile.

"I'm not sure that would stand up in a court of law," George said before finishing the last bite of donut, "but I surely appreciate the sentiment."

"Then I hope it never comes up in court," I answered. "How about another donut for the road?"

The mayor looked tempted, but ultimately he shook his head in the negative. "Thanks, but I'd better not. I'll pass the word along around town that you're open, if you'd like me to."

"That would be great," I said as I collected his money and made his change. "Thanks for coming by. I trust that I'll see you later, Mr. Mayor."

"Sometime, but maybe not for a while," George said.

"You don't have to wait for Polly to go somewhere else before you come see me, even if you don't order any donuts while you're here," I said.

"I realize that, but we both know that it's too tempting for me to come in here if I can't get *anything*."

"There's always our coffee."

"True, but it goes so much better with a donut, don't you think?"

"My entire business plan depends on it," I said as I transferred his remaining coffee into a paper cup, topped it off, and then put a lid on it before I handed it back to him.

I wasn't sure who all he told, or how he got the word out, but soon enough, we were inundated with customers again. I'd have to treat him to a free donut the next time he came in, whether Polly approved of the gesture or not.

After all, George and I had been friends a lot longer than the man had been dating his secretary.

Time flew quickly for the next few hours, and we were closing the donut shop before I knew it. It had taken a little time for Sharon and me to get into the swing of things working together, but by the time we were finished for the day, we were nearly flawlessly in sync.

"Thanks for coming in today," I told her as I let her out the front door. "You were a great help."

"I don't mind staying and helping you tidy up here," she said.

"I appreciate the offer, but I'm nearly finished myself. Do you know if you'll be in tomorrow?"

"That really all depends on Emma. If she's up to coming in, I won't try to keep her from it, but if not, you can count on me. I'll be here again bright and early."

"It's good to be able to count on you both," I said.

"Hey, it's a lot of fun as long as you don't have to do it every day," Sharon said, and then an instant later, she quickly added, "Not that I don't think it's fun for you."

"No worries. I knew what you meant," I said with a smile. "Sometimes it can be a grind, but most days I love what I do."

"Then you're in the right business," she said with a laugh.

After Sharon was gone, I finished balancing the register receipts versus the cash on hand and was pleased to find them in complete agreement. It always made me feel warm and fuzzy inside when that happened.

I was just finishing up the deposit slip for the day when someone started knocking on the front door. I was still a good five minutes away from being finished, so it appeared that Grace was there early.

When I looked up, though, it wasn't Grace standing there trying to get my attention.

It was the police chief, instead, and from the expression on his face, he wasn't there to share good news.

I couldn't help wondering what he wanted as I made my way to the door. He knew that Grace and I were digging into Rick Hastings' murder, so that couldn't be it. Besides, we hadn't even had a chance to turn over the first leaf yet.

But clearly something had the man out of sorts, and I had a hunch that I was about to find out exactly what it might be.

Chapter 6

"What can I do for you, Chief?" I asked him as I held the door open.

"Suzanne, I hate to bother you during your regular business hours about something that's personal," he started off saying, and I felt pure relief. I'd been afraid that the reason for his visit had something to do with me, but I was pretty certain now that it was something else entirely.

"It's no bother at all. Would you like a donut?" I asked him half-joking, knowing that his answer would be no. Before he'd started seeing my mother, his waistline had been ample enough for two men, but since then, he'd steadfastly refused my offerings, and had pared down accordingly.

"Sure, why not? I'll have one with chocolate icing and sprinkles, too," he said a little sadly.

I nearly fell over when I heard his request. "I'm not in the habit of discouraging my customers from ordering treats, but are you sure that you want to do that?"

The police chief seemed to think about it for a few seconds, and then he shook his head. "You're right. I'd better not. Does that tell you anything about how upset I am?"

"If I weren't taking you seriously before, you've certainly got my attention now. What exactly can I do for you?"

"It's about your mother," he said with a frown.

I couldn't keep myself from groaning the second I heard him mention Momma.

"I know, it's not fair to involve you in this, but I don't know where else to turn," he continued.

"I understand. Talk to me," I said as I sat on our most comfortable couch and patted the seat beside me.

"You really don't mind?"

"Well, I'm honestly not sure that I'll be of much help, but at least I'm a good listener," I said. The last thing I wanted to do was to get between a man and his wife. It was bad enough that the wife in this case was my very own mother, but the fact that they were still newlyweds made it that much harder. I didn't remember any time being married to Max, my ex, as particularly blissful, but the first year was by far the worst of all of the time that we spent together. Well, catching him cheating on me with another woman wasn't a picnic either, but the sentiment was true just the same.

"Thanks. I appreciate that," he said, the relief clear in his voice. "The honest truth is that I don't think she's very happy about me staying on as chief of police. She doesn't want me working anymore."

That didn't sound like my mother at all. "Did she actually say that to you?"

"No, not in so many words, but I can tell from the way that she's been acting, you know?"

I shook my head. "Chief, I'd love to help you, but it's pretty clear to me that you're talking to the wrong woman. If you want to know how my momma is feeling about anything, and I mean anything, then you need to ask her directly yourself."

The chief looked uncomfortable for a moment before he spoke again. "But what if I'm afraid to?" he asked me, his voice barely above a whisper.

The admission caught me off-guard. "Why on earth is that? She's a reasonable woman. If you ask her what's wrong, I'm willing to bet that she'll tell you."

"Suzanne, the fact is that I'd rather face an armed felon than ask your mother a question that I'm not sure what the answer is."

"Sorry, but I can't help you there. I will say that I can't imagine anything that she has to say being worse than what you're already imagining."

"But what if it is?"

"Then at least you'll know what you're dealing with and can go from there," I responded.

The chief pondered that for a few seconds, and then he nodded. "You're right. That's solid advice. Thanks."

"Don't mention it," I said. I wanted to ask him what else

he'd discovered about Rick Hastings' murder, but I didn't feel right taking advantage of the situation. After all, he'd come to me for help, and I just couldn't bring myself to violate that.

It turned out that I didn't have to, though.

On his way out the door, the chief paused, then he looked directly back at me. "You didn't hear this from me, but Hastings died from a knife wound to the heart. It was a quick way to go, for what it's worth. I doubt that he felt much pain in the end."

"So then most likely he was murdered on the spot," I said. "If that's true, then how could someone not have seen it happen?"

The chief said, "I've been asking myself that very same question. Even as we speak, I've got my men searching for any footage from Spirit Night from folks who were there. Maybe someone caught something suspicious on tape and they don't even realize it."

"I hope you're right," I said. "Thanks for trusting me with the information. I promise that I won't tell anyone but Grace."

Chief Martin shrugged. "You don't have to keep it quiet on my account. Ray Blake somehow got ahold of the news, so everybody in town probably knows it by now. I take it you don't read the morning paper."

"We were too busy working to even look at it this morning," I said.

He looked surprised by that bit of news. "We? Does that mean that Emma actually came in to work today?"

"No, but Sharon was here substituting for her. She didn't mention anything about it, but then again, I doubt that Ray even told her. It's an odd relationship the two of them have."

"If I've learned anything over the years, it's that each marriage is different in its own way," the chief said. "Thanks again for the advice."

"Good luck with Momma," I said, and then I let him out.

"I hope I don't need it, but thanks for the sentiment

anyway."

"Don't worry. I'm sure that everything will be just fine," I said, trying to give him as much encouragement as I could.

"Absolutely," he replied, but there was little conviction in it.

The chief was clearly distracted by his misunderstanding with my mother, and I could dwell on it myself if I let it, but I had a murder to investigate. After all, I wasn't a relationship counselor. Then again, I wasn't a homicide detective either, but at least I had a little experience tracking down killers, and I would rather do that than butt into my mother's brand-new marriage.

"Are you ready to go?" Grace asked me when she showed up at Donut Hearts five minutes after the chief left.

"I'm just about done here," I said as I completed totaling the day's receipts. We'd started off slowly but we'd finished strong, and I was glad that I'd kept the shop open after all. Even after paying Emma *and* her mother, I'd made enough to keep the wolves at bay for at least one more day, and that was pure gold as far as I was concerned.

"Super. Now, if we only knew where to start digging," Grace said as she took a seat near the register and watched me finish my paperwork.

"It just so happens that we do. Sharon worked with me this morning instead of Emma, and she had some interesting insights about Rick Hastings and the folks he hung out with. We've got four very solid leads to pursue."

"Excellent," Grace answered. "I do wish we knew how he died, though. That could really help our investigation."

"I know that," I responded. "I take it that you haven't read today's paper, either."

"I find the news too depressing to deal with the first thing in the morning," Grace replied. "Why, did I miss an ad, or a coupon, or something?"

"Actually, I just heard that Ray published the cause of death in his paper. Rick Hastings was stabbed once through the heart. He died almost instantly."

"Then it had to have happened in front of everyone in the park," Grace said. "Who has that kind of luck?"

"What do you mean? I wouldn't call dying from a stab wound all that lucky."

"I was talking about the killer getting away with it. We both know from personal experience that the park was crowded last night. How could no one have seen what happened?"

"The police force is going around trying to collect videos and photographs of the event last night. Chief Martin is hoping to catch something that the person doing the filming might have missed."

Grace's left eyebrow lifted for a moment. "Is the chief actually confiding in you now?"

"He was here for something else," I explained. "The news he gave me about Rick Hastings was almost an afterthought."

"That sounds potentially juicy. Why did he come by Donut Hearts in the first place?"

I just shrugged. "It was just some family stuff. You understand why I shouldn't say anything more."

"Completely," Grace replied with a smile, dropping it instantly. I could have said something to her about my discussion with the chief, but on impulse I'd decided to keep family problems just that, in the family, and while it was true that Grace was my best friend and a sister from another mother, I still didn't feel right sharing the chief's concerns about my own mother with her. I just felt fortunate that my best friend understood and accepted my reticence. "So," Grace said as she rubbed her hands together. "Let's hear about this list of suspects."

I pulled out the sheet of paper Sharon had given me and handed it to her. "I can do better than that. I can let you see it for yourself."

Grace took it from me and studied the names Emma's mother had written down before looking up at me. "I don't know Denny West, do you?"

"He's the one mystery on the list to me, as well," I said. "Should we tackle him first, or leave him for last?"

"I say we approach the three devils we know before we go after the one that we don't," Grace said. "Is that okay with you?"

"Honestly, I'm not all that particular on where we get started. Let's stop by the bank and drop my deposit off first, and then we can begin sleuthing."

Grace nodded, and then I saw her staring out the front window for a moment before she spoke again. "Suzanne, can your deposit wait?"

"I suppose so," I said, curious about her request. "Is there any reason in particular you don't want to go by the bank first?"

"Isn't that Kyle's landscaping truck parked near The Boxcar Grill? If we hurry, we might be able to catch him before he leaves. We can always do your deposit later."

I shoved the cash, the credit card receipts, and the deposit slip into a bank bag and practically shoved Grace out the front door. "What are we waiting for? Let's go!"

We didn't even get inside the diner before Kyle Creasy met us as he trotted down the front steps. "Excuse me, ladies," he said as he tried to brush past us. Kyle was in his late twenties, but his receding hairline and his weatherworn face belied that fact. His khaki outfit was stained a few places with dirt and grass, but the blemishes almost looked as though they were parts of his uniform.

"Kyle, do you have a second?" I asked him as I turned and followed him back down the steps.

"What's up, Suzanne?" Before I could tell him, he added, "I haven't been by the donut shop lately because I'm trying to lose a few pounds. Once I get started on your treats, I have a hard time saying no."

"It's not about that," I said. "Grace and I would love to talk to you about Rick Hastings."

Kyle's face shifted into neutral mode the second he heard

the man's name. "Sorry, but I can't help you."

"You're not saying that you didn't know him, are you?" Grace asked him pointedly.

"No, and don't put words into my mouth," Kyle said a little hotly. "I knew Rick, but I can't say that I'm sorry that he's gone. He was a troublemaker, and he toyed with people's affections; I don't have any patience for that kind of person."

"Exactly how was he a troublemaker for you?" I asked.

"The man was constantly sticking his nose where it didn't belong," Kyle explained. "I'm not even all that surprised that he met the end that he did."

"That's kind of harsh, isn't it?" I asked him.

"I know that I'm not supposed to speak ill of the dead, so sue me."

"He clearly was on your bad side," Grace said. "We're both just wondering why."

Kyle took a khaki baseball hat from his back pocket, creased the brim once down the middle, and then firmly wedged it into place onto his head. "Why is that?"

"Why is what?" I asked.

"Why do you two want to know?"

I thought about lying to him, but just as quickly, I decided to tell him the truth. "We're trying to find out who killed him."

Grace frowned at me, but Kyle did not. "I get it. You're doing it for Emma, aren't you?"

I just shrugged. "Why we're doing it isn't really all that important."

"I'm not sure that Emma would agree with you, but that's none of my business," Kyle said. "The next time you see her, you should tell that girl that she's better off without that snake in her life, even though she might not realize it yet. Give her some time and distance, though, and she'll come around; I guarantee it. There are a lot better choices than she even realizes right under her own nose."

"You're not sweet on her yourself, are you?" Grace asked him.

Kyle's face immediately flushed. "That's nobody's business but my own. Now I've got to go. I'm going to be late as it is."

After Kyle was gone, I asked Grace, "How did you know that he liked Emma?"

"It was just a hunch. He sounded a little too overprotective of her to me when he talked about her, don't you think?"

"Maybe, now that you mention it. That's good detective work, Grace."

She saluted me as she added with a smile, "Happy to be of service, ma'am."

"You can knock off the sarcasm," I said with a grin. "I was complimenting you."

"I know, and I appreciate it. Could that be why Kyle might have gotten rid of Rick? Was he making room in Emma's life for himself?"

"There are easier ways to do that than killing her current boyfriend," I said.

"Maybe so, but nothing is nearly as effective."

"True," I said. "I want to speak with him again later, but for now, I think we should find Travis or Amanda. Any thoughts about them?"

"Flip a coin. I'm feeling lucky either way."

I considered sharing Emma's mother's definition of luck with Grace, but ultimately I decided to keep it to myself.

If what Grace had done had been just luck, I hoped that we were in store for a lot more of it before our investigation was over.

Chapter 7

"Travis, do you have a second?" I asked the construction company owner after Grace and I walked into his small trailer. It was obvious that this was his home base, and I had a hunch that it traveled with him as well when he was on a big job. In one corner were a cot, a hot plate, and a small loveseat, while in the other there stood a desk and three chairs. Everything looked crammed into the small space, and I didn't know how anyone would ever get any work done there. I knew that I'd get claustrophobic in a minute if I had to stay there very long. Then again, I knew that the hours I worked at Donut Hearts would drive most folks quickly out of the donutmaking business, so we each had our own limitations that we were willing to deal with. I'd heard that Travis had two employees, but they must have been out on smaller jobs, because we found him there alone, which was a good thing. I doubted that all five of us would have been able to breathe inside, and at least one of us would have had to sit on the cot.

"Do you need a job done, Suzanne?" Travis asked hopefully. "That cottage of yours is ripe for a remodel, and my team is perfect for the job."

"My cottage is fine just the way it is, thank you very much," I said, probably a little curter than I should have been.

"Then the donut shop? I'm not sure what you had in mind, but we can make it work. I guarantee it."

"Donut Hearts is perfect just the way it stands," I said a little snippily.

"Hey, no offense intended," Travis said. He was a big man with scarred meaty hands that testified to his time working construction. To counter his rough exterior, Travis had done his best to cultivate a "good old boy" attitude nearly to perfection, but I could see the hard edge just beneath the surface. "Do you need something then, Grace?"

"Actually, I've been playing around with the idea of adding a wing to the back of my house," she said, catching me off-guard completely. Was it actually true, or was she just using this wild idea as an excuse to speak with the construction company owner?

"Seriously? You've come to the right place. I'm pretty booked right now, but I might be able to fit you in, being how you're a friend and all." I glanced over at Travis whiteboard display and saw that the three jobs listed there were all crossed off. If he had any work at all scheduled, it wasn't readily apparent from his list.

"Honestly, I'm more in the planning phase right now," she said. "In the meantime, we'd like to talk to you about Rick Hastings, though."

For a moment Travis' nice exterior slipped, revealing an angry burst toward the deceased rival. "I don't know what Rick might have told you, but I can promise you that whatever it is, it's not true."

"Really," Grace said, keeping her expression level.

Travis' face just seemed to brighten even more. "Bring him over here right now. We'll see if he'll say to my face whatever it is that he told you. One thing is for sure: I don't owe him one thin dime, and that's the truth."

"Okay. Sure," I said, adding a tone to my voice that implied I was skeptical about his statement.

The results were even better than I'd been hoping for. "I made the deal without his help! He came sniffing around for a commission, and I sent him packing. He didn't like it, and he wouldn't leave. I gave him a little help out the door, and now he's going around claiming that I assaulted him. Let me clue you in about something. Rick implied that if I paid him money I didn't owe him, he'd make everything else go away, including the complaint he was about to swear out on me. People have tried to muscle me around before, and it's never worked out well for them. I expect Rick to drop his phony story soon enough, but in the meantime, that shouldn't keep you from using me as your contractor. If you need a good architect, I've got a guy that I can recommend who's gangbusters, and we make a great team."

It was time to step in and tell Travis about Rick. If his behavior was legitimate, he didn't know that his accuser was dead. "You haven't heard the news, have you?"

"I don't know what you're talking about. I've been holed up in here for the past two days eating out of my fridge and sleeping on the cot to get a bid ready for a big job in Charlotte." He shuffled a few papers, and then he said, "If your job isn't that high a priority, I need to get my bid in by five."

"Rick Hastings was murdered last night," I said, watching Travis' face as I spoke.

The builder looked at me sharply before he spoke. "Murdered? No way."

"It's true," Grace said. "Did anyone see you here last night around dusk?"

Travis bit his lower lip, and then he stood, filling part of the trailer with his bulk. "You're asking me for an alibi? Really? I told you, I was here alone."

"So you say," Grace said.

Travis was clearly about to lash out at her when he suddenly had a change of heart. In a calm voice, he told us, "Like I said, I've got to get this bid done soon or I'm going to lose the job. If you decide to do your project later, let me know, Grace."

Travis walked us out of the trailer, and then locked the door behind us after we were outside. I would have liked to speak with him a little longer, but it wasn't as though we'd had any choice in leaving.

As we were walking back to my Jeep, I asked Grace, "Since when have you been thinking about expanding? You're rattling around in that big house by yourself as it is. What on earth do you need more room for?"

Grace grinned at me. "I have no idea. It just came to me, and it seemed like a good idea at the time. My, Travis has a bit of a temper, doesn't he?"

"He tries to project a genial façade to the world, but I'd hate to cross him."

"Do you mean like Rick Hastings did?" Grace asked me. "I can't believe that Travis told us all of that about their squabbles."

"Maybe he knew that we'd find out sooner or later, so he went ahead and laid it out for us himself," I said. "It would be a savvy thing to do."

"Maybe so, but does Travis strike you as the shrewd type?" Grace asked me.

"I don't know yet. He's hard to read."

"At any rate, we have a pair of motives for him now."

It was time to ask her something that I'd been dreading. "Grace, do you have any problem with me sharing what we've learned so far with the police chief?"

"No, by all means, tell him everything. I fully realize that we entered a new stage the day he married your mother. Who knows? Maybe it will help him in his investigation."

I dialed the chief's number, but it went straight to voicemail. I left a message. "This is Suzanne. Call when you get a chance. No urgency, I just want to bring you up to speed."

"He didn't answer," I said as I put my phone away.

"So I gathered. Now what?"

I thought about it, and then I said, "Well, we can speak with Amanda if we can find her, or we can try to track down Denny West."

"Do you mind if we grab a bite to eat first?" Grace asked. "I'm starving."

"Sure. How's the Boxcar sound? I know we made it part of the way up the steps earlier. Maybe this time we can make it all the way inside."

Grace grinned. "I *love* Trish's food. Let's go. Maybe while we're there, we'll be able to figure out how we're going to find our last two suspects."

"We could always just ask Trish," I suggested as we got into my Jeep and drove over to the diner. "After all, she knows just about everybody around town."

"If they live around here in the first place," Grace said.

"If they don't, I'm sure that we'll have friends in other places who might be able to help us. Between the two of us, we know a lot of people in our part of North Carolina."

"Then again, we could always just do an Internet search on my phone," Grace suggested.

"I suppose we could approach it that way, but what fun would that be?"

"Is that why we're doing this; for fun?" my best friend asked me.

"No, I realize more than most that this is serious business. Go on. Work your Internet magic and find out all you can about Amanda and Denny."

"I'm on it," Grace said as she started typing into her cellphone. Grace was a whiz at Internet searches, and while I appreciated the technology and her mastery of it, I basically just used my phone to make calls and send texts. Then again, I had a pretty basic unit, while Grace's company provided her with advanced equipment that was up to date and capable of running the Space Shuttle, for all I knew.

"Hey there," Trish said as Grace and I walked in a few minutes later. "Didn't I see you two outside earlier?"

"Wow, you don't miss a beat, do you?" I asked her with a smile. "Yes, we were here, but we suddenly got distracted."

"I saw you talking to Kyle. What was that about?"

Did this woman miss anything within her realm? I just shrugged. "You know, just stuff."

Trish lowered her voice and took a step closer. "You two are investigating Rick's murder, aren't you?"

I looked around and saw a few customers listening to us intently, though they pretended not to be. April Springs was a small town, and while I usually loved that fact, sometimes it could be a nuisance having everyone know my business. Instead of answering, I winked at her, hoping that no one else could see it.

"Got it. Touch base with me later," Trish whispered. "Sit anywhere; one place is as good as the next," she added loudly, and Grace followed me to a table against the back wall. It was the only chance we'd have any privacy at all in the dining car, and I still didn't like our odds.

A minute later, Trish showed up with two glasses of iced sweet tea. "I took a guess about what you wanted to drink. Is sweet tea okay?"

"Better than okay," I said as I took a sip of mine. The cool purity of the sweetened tea slid down beautifully, and I quickly took another, bigger sip. "That's wonderful."

"We aim to please. What's Grace so wrapped up in?" Trish asked as she topped off my glass.

I was about to answer when my friend did it herself. "It's just work stuff," she replied as she glanced up and smiled at Trish. "Suzanne can order for me, too. I'll have whatever she's having."

It was my turn to grin now. "Wow, I could be really mean right now, but I think I'll stick to the usual: a cheeseburger and fries, please."

Grace looked up again long enough to hold two fingers up in the air. "Like I said, make that two."

"Coming right up," Trish said, and then she walked back up front to where the kitchen connected to the dining room, her ever-present ponytail bobbing with every step that she took.

"Any luck yet?" I asked Grace softly.

"Some. I need a little more time, though."

"Sorry," I said quickly.

"No worries, my friend."

I was about to reply when Gabby Williams, the woman who owned ReNEWed, a gently used clothing store, approached my table. Without a moment of pleasantries, she asked bluntly, "So, when's the big wedding?"

I was so caught unaware that I actually asked her, "What wedding?"

Gabby grimaced a little, her natural, fallback expression

most of the time. "Yours."

"To be honest with you, we haven't even talked about setting a date yet," I answered.

"What are you waiting for? You're not getting any younger, you know."

I could usually handle Gabby's impertinence, but for some reason, it struck me as being even ruder than normal. "As a matter of fact, neither are you."

I heard a gasp a few tables beyond her, but I chose to ignore it. It could go either way now. Either Gabby would unleash her fury on me for my boldness, or she'd let it slide and pretend that I hadn't said anything.

To my surprise, she chose a third option. After letting out a startling laugh that got everyone's attention, she smiled as she said, "Too true. The reason I ask is that I just got a wedding gown in that will fit you perfectly, if you're interested."

"Is it white?" I asked her, still startled by her amiable response. Maybe she was one of those folks who just loved weddings, though I never would have predicted it based on her past behavior.

"Of course it is."

"Well, that might be a problem, then. After all, I'm not exactly a blushing innocent," I said. "I've been married before, remember? How appropriate would it be for me to wear white again?"

"You're kidding, right? I had a customer who bought a new gown from me every three years for twelve years running, each one whiter than the one before."

"Well, I imagine that I'll wear a nice pantsuit, or maybe even a dress, instead of a formal gown," I said.

"I have those, too, you know. I'll keep my eye out for something you'll like."

"Thanks," I said.

"Happy to do it." A little wistfully, she added, "I just love a good wedding."

So, that particular theory had just been confirmed, much to

my surprise. "I'll be sure to let you know as soon as I'm ready to shop for something."

"Fine."

Our food came as Gabby left, and as Trish placed our orders in front of us, she asked, "What was that all about?"

"Gabby wanted me to look at a wedding dress that she just got into the shop," I said with a smile.

"Are you seriously thinking about wearing a formal white bridal gown, Suzanne?" Trish asked.

"Not a chance. If I did wear one, it would be more for the irony of it, and there's not going to be a single thing to mock when I marry Jake." I studied the food. "This looks perfect."

"It better be," Trish said.

"Grace, our food's here," I said as I picked up a fry and ate it.

"One second," she said, and then she turned back to her screen.

"No hurry. I'll be happy to wait," I said as I picked up my burger and took a rather large and unladylike bite from it.

"There's no need to do that for me," she said, and then she looked at me with a grin, spotting the bite that I'd just taken. "Why am I not surprised?"

"Hey, I said that I was hungry, too. Did you have any luck?"

Grace started to say something when she looked around and saw several folks still watching and listening to every word we were saying, and yet trying their best not to be noticed doing it. "After."

"Then let's eat," I said, agreeing with the sentiment.

As we dined on that glorious meal, I couldn't help but think about what Gabby had suggested. On the face of it, wearing white was ridiculous, even if I was starting my life over with Jake by my side. I'd loved to play pretend as a girl as much as any other girl I knew had, but this was not fantasy. Marrying the man of my dreams, as corny as that might have sounded if I'd said it out loud, was the reality, and it was so much better than any scenario I might have dreamed up as a child.

After we ate and paid for our meals, Grace and I lingered at the register for a second. I'd tried to get Trish's attention, since she'd asked me to touch base with her at some point, but she was busy dealing with a group of other customers. I caught her eye and held up my thumb and pinkie, imitating a telephone, as I mouthed the words, call me.

She nodded, and Grace and I left.

"That was perfect," I said. "Now back to business. Did you have any luck finding either one of our last two suspects?"

"It was tough, but I finally got a line on both of them."

"Let's hear what you've got," I said as we headed for my Jeep, now ready to tackle the world again after filling our bellies.

Grace was interrupted before she had a chance to get started, though, as my cellphone rang.

"It's Chief Martin," I told her after glancing at the caller ID, and then I answered. "Hi. Thanks for calling me back."

"Suzanne, I need you to come to my office at the police station right now."

"Does it have to be this instant? Grace and I are busy at the moment."

"Sorry, but this can't wait. You should come alone, so ask Grace if she could meet up with you later," the chief said.

"Is that an order?" I asked, resenting his command.

There was a heavy sigh on the other end of the line, and then Chief Martin asked me in a voice full of contrition, "Just do this for me without giving me any grief, okay?"

"Fine. I'll see you in a few minutes," I said. I'd never heard him couch a request like that, and I wanted to see what this was all about.

"What's up?" Grace asked me as I put my cellphone back in my pocket.

"There's been a sudden change of plans. I need to drop

you off at home, if you don't mind. The chief wants to see me in his office right away."

"Without me?" Grace asked, clearly unhappy about being left out.

"I'm sorry, but I have a hunch that if I don't go alone, I'm not going to find out what's happening," I explained. "Do this for me, could you? Is there anything that you can do for an hour while I see what's going on at the police station?"

She shrugged. "Actually, I've got a pile of paperwork waiting for me, but I'd still rather go with you."

"That's my preference, too, but I didn't get a choice."

After a few seconds, Grace finally gave in. "Fine, but you need to come by my place the second you leave the station and tell me everything that happened. Is that agreed?"

"Agreed," I said.

We got to her place quickly, and I let her out. As I drove back toward the chief's office, I couldn't help but wonder what this sudden summons was all about. Knowing that I'd find out in a few minutes didn't make it any easier to take, either.

When I drove up, I saw him standing out in front of the precinct door, and by the expression on his face, I had a hunch that I wasn't going to like what was about to come next.

The way it ended up, boy, was that ever the truth.

Chapter 8

"I'm out here because I wanted to speak with you first," the chief told me after I'd parked my Jeep in one of the spaces out front. He'd met me halfway in the parking lot, and his expression hadn't softened during his stroll over.

"What's going on? Nothing's wrong with Momma, is it?"

"No, of course not. Why would you even think that?"

"Well, even you have to admit that this is all kind of mysterious," I said.

"No worries on that front. Your mother is fine."

"Have you spoken with her yet about what's been troubling her lately?" I asked him.

"That's why I asked you to come by. Suzanne, I've officially resigned, once and for all, as the chief of police for April Springs."

"I already knew that," I replied. "You're still going to keep filling in until Jake can finish working his notice so he can decide if he wants to take over, right?"

"I'm sorry, but it looks as though that's not going to happen. I've already spoken with Jake this morning, and so has the mayor. It appears that he meant what he said before. Jake made it pretty clear that he's not interested in my job, and I can't take another second of it."

"Hang on a second and give me a chance to talk to him before you do anything rash," I said, almost pleading with my stepfather. If Jake would leave the state police and become our new police chief, everything would be pretty much ideal for us.

At least that's what I believed.

"Call him and see for yourself, Suzanne."

I did as the chief requested, and Jake answered on the first ring. "I just have one question for you. Did you turn down the chief of police job?" I asked him before he had the chance to even say hello.

"Suzanne, I told you all along that I wasn't interested in

taking over there. Phillip clearly needs to move on, but I'm not going to be the one who takes his place."

Jake had already told me that more than once over the past several days, but that clearly didn't mean that I'd accepted it. "Think about it before you do anything rash, Jake. It would be perfect."

"Not for me. I'm sorry. Suzanne, I hate to disappoint you, but it's not going to happen," he said flatly, and I knew that it was true, no matter how much I wished that it might be otherwise. "Do you still love me, anyway?" he asked in a softer voice.

"Only with all my heart," I said. "I didn't mean to push you so hard. If it's not right for you, then it's not right."

The relief was clear in his voice as he replied, "I'm not saying never; I'm just saying not right now."

"Got it."

"Listen, I hate to do this, but I really have to go," Jake said.

"Go. We'll talk later."

"I'll call you tonight if I can," Jake answered, and I hung up, still a little stunned by the police chief's sudden departure. I knew that he'd been threatening to leave since his brother's untimely demise, but a part of me hadn't believed it.

I asked the chief, "What made you decide to act so suddenly? I thought you were planning to hang on for a while."

"We both know that there's nothing sudden about it," the chief said. "In a way, this is all your fault."

"How's that possible?" I asked him, not understanding what he meant.

"Well, I took your advice and spoke with your mother. She was upset that I was still working as the police chief, even after I'd promised to quit. She told me that if I was going to leave, I needed to do it now. The more I thought about it, the more I agreed with her. I've been miserable just hanging around waiting for someone to step in and take over. I told the mayor my decision, and an hour later, he had my replacement lined up, effective immediately."

"He's already hired someone!" I asked shrilly.

"There was no need to dawdle. My mind was made up, so there was no use delaying the inevitable."

"Did he at least promote from within?" I asked, hoping that Grace's boyfriend, Officer Stephen Grant, might have inherited the job.

"No, he's hired an officer from the Granite Meadows Police Force. The man's supposed to be good, and what's even more important, he can start immediately."

"If he's so good, how can he just leave his old job without at least giving them any notice?" I asked.

"I pulled some strings to make it happen," George said as he and a stranger approached us. "The mayor there owed me a favor, so he intervened with the police chief. Let's go to Phillip's office where we can discuss this in private."

"Hey, it's not my office anymore," Chief, or Former Chief Martin, said. "Ask Chief Tyler."

"It's not official until tomorrow at eight AM, so you might as well call me Alex until then," the new chief said. He was tall and lean, somewhere in his mid-thirties, I'd say if I had to guess. There was a scar on his left cheek, and he had a full head of brown hair, and icy dark eyes that were almost black.

"That's just a formality, as far as I'm concerned," the chief said.

"I don't want to go anywhere," I said stubbornly, still reeling from shock about how quickly things had just changed.

"Suzanne, we couldn't wait on Jake forever," George said. "He told me himself that he didn't want the job, and I had to do something, for the town's sake."

"I get it," I said. "I just didn't think that it would all happen so fast."

"There wasn't much choice. Anyway, we all thought you deserved to know about it before it became official."

"Thanks for that much, anyway," I said.

"May I have a word with you in private?" the new chief

asked me softly. I didn't like the look in his eyes, and I couldn't read his expression.

"Actually, anything you have to say to me you can say in front of my stepfather and the mayor," I said. Let him try to isolate me from my support and see where it got him.

"As you wish. I understand that you consider yourself somewhat of an amateur sleuth."

"I've never called myself that," I said.

The new chief shrugged. "But it's true nonetheless, isn't it? While my predecessor here may have allowed you some latitude investigating crime as a private citizen, be warned that I will not. In my opinion, there's no room in police business for a rank amateur."

"That's a little harsh, don't you think?" Chief Martin asked.

Chief Tyler stared at him for a second before he spoke. "I'm not surprised that you feel that way, given that she's your stepdaughter, but that doesn't make any difference to me. I won't have her muddying the waters in any of my investigations."

"Hang on a second," George said in an amiable manner. "Maybe we've all gotten off on the wrong foot here. Chief Tyler, you should know that Suzanne is a valued member of our community."

"I don't doubt it, but unless she's carrying a badge, she's just going to get in my way. Your honor, you might not like the way I run the department, but I can't take orders from you. You can change your mind about hiring me, or fire me later at any point you wish, but you might as well know up front that you can't tell me what to do, or how I should run my department."

I half-expected George to cut him loose on the spot, but to my surprise, he merely nodded. "The point is a valid one. After all, it's your department."

"Thanks for nothing, old friend," I said to him, and then I stormed off back to my Jeep.

"Suzanne, let me explain," George said as he started to follow me.

The mayor might have had a perfectly rational reason for behaving the way he just had, but that didn't mean that I had to like it, or even make nice with the new chief of police after the scolding that I'd just received. Chief Tyler had made it pretty clear that he didn't care all that much about my opinion, so why should I care about his?

As I drove past the three of them, I saw Chief Martin mouth the word "Sorry" in my direction, but I didn't offer him any response, or even acknowledgment.

I was too mad to trust myself.

Things had suddenly been turned upside down, but there was at least one comfort in what had just happened.

I still had until the next morning to find Rick Hastings' killer before I had to worry about the wrath of Chief Tyler, and I meant to get busy. If it meant that Grace and I had to stay up all night tracking down the killer, then we would just have to do our best.

It might be a long shot, given the current state of our investigation, but it was all of the time that we had left, and I meant to make the most of it.

"So, what was the big secret?" Grace asked me as I walked up the steps to her front porch. She was out there waiting for me, but I wasn't all that eager to deliver the news I'd just received, especially not after the reception I'd just been given by the new police chief.

"Apparently there's a new sheriff in town," I said, trying to lighten my message.

"Suzanne, we don't have a sheriff," Grace said as my humor fell flat.

"We both know that I meant chief of police. Apparently, Chief Martin has officially stepped down, or he will tomorrow at eight AM, and George has already hired someone to take his place."

"Is it Jake?"

"No," I said.

A hopeful look shot through her gaze. "Stephen?"

"Again, no."

"Who is it, then?"

"Some guy named Alex Tyler," I replied. "He's been working in Granite Meadows, but come tomorrow morning, he's going to be our problem."

"What's he like?" Grace asked me.

"Well, to begin with, he told me that our time as unofficial investigators was about to be over."

My best friend looked surprised by the news. "He can't do that, can he?"

"Evidently he can."

"Don't worry. George will step up for us," Grace said confidently.

"Grace, the man was standing right there when Chief Tyler read me the riot act, and so was my stepfather. Neither one of them lifted a finger in our defense. It looks as though we're about to be out of business."

"Suzanne, we can't just take this lying down. We have to fight back."

I shook my head as I answered, "What are we supposed to do? He's going to be the one in charge around here. He told the mayor right in front of me that George could fire him, but he couldn't tell him what to do, and our old friend agreed with him."

"That doesn't sound like George, letting this guy just roll over us like that," Grace said.

"Whether we like it or not, I have to grudgingly admit that he's got a point."

"Chief Tyler?" Grace asked me incredulously.

"No, of course not. I'm talking about George. He hired this man to run the department, so he can't very well dictate terms to him."

"So then we're just giving up?" Grace asked as she stared hard at me.

"Not on your life. We have two more suspects to speak with, and until tomorrow morning, we can do whatever we choose to without asking anyone for permission."

"Then what are we waiting for?" Grace asked as she jumped up. "Let's get cracking."

"What did you uncover about Amanda and Denny?" I asked as I joined her at my Jeep.

"Apparently Amanda works at an auto repair shop in Union Square."

"She's a mechanic?" I asked her, startled by the thought of it.

"No, not that there would be anything wrong with it if she were."

"Of course not. What does she do there, then?"

"She's the office manager," Grace said, and then she frowned slightly. "In all honesty, I don't know who actually owns the place. There are some shell companies holding the incorporation papers, but I couldn't figure out where they ultimately led."

"Maybe we'll ask her when we see her," I suggested.

"We can always try, but I doubt that she'll tell us, not after someone went to so much trouble to hide the fact on paper."

"How about Denny?" I asked.

"I found out that he lives in Union Square, too, but I still can't figure out what he does for a living. From what I've been able to gather, he makes his money in the shadows, much like Rick Hastings did."

"How have these men been able to make a living?"

"From what I've been able to gather, it's mostly been from extortion, gambling, and other shady activities," Grace said.

"Boy, Emma sure knows how to pick them, doesn't she?"

"Don't be too hard on her. At least she has her youth as an excuse. I've dated more than my share of bad men in the past, and what's more, I'm old enough to know better."

I knew that Grace had endured a string of bad boyfriends over the years, but I wasn't about to find fault with her. She'd always followed her heart instead of her head, even though it had led her down more than her share of dead ends in the past. "You've found a good guy now though, haven't you?"

"I have indeed," she said.

"Do you mind if I ask you something?"

Grace just smiled. "Would it matter if I said yes?"

"Not too much, but you can always feel free to ignore the question."

"Go on, then," she said.

I had to word this just so, but it was something that I'd been wondering about ever since my best friend had started dating the young cop. "Do you ever get bored with the fact that Stephen Grant is a good guy with no real drama in his life?"

Grace laughed. "Are you kidding? He's a breath of fresh air. I don't know why people say that nice guys finish last. I never fully appreciated how lovely it could be to have someone in my life who actually puts my needs ahead of his own. I wouldn't trade him for a thousand bad boys, and that's the truth."

"Good for you," I said.

"You should be proud, Suzanne. After all, I'm just following your example."

What a curious thing to say. "How so?"

"You went from Max, a born womanizer with very few redeeming qualities, to a state police inspector. That's a pretty dramatic shift you've gone through yourself."

"Max was never that bad, even at his worst," I said, defending my ex for some odd reason.

"Come on. He cheated on you, Suzanne, or have you forgotten about that?"

"You don't have to remind me, but he's changed, Grace. You've seen him with Emily. It's clear that man adores her, and he'd never do anything to hurt her."

"Actually, I've been wondering something myself, since we're having a frank chat. How does that make you feel?" Grace asked as we got into the Jeep and started the drive toward Union Square.

"I'm happy for both of them," I said, keeping my gaze

directed to the road ahead of us.

"Are you saying that you're not the least little bit jealous?"

"Of them? No, that thought never crossed my mind."

"That's because you're a better person than I am," she said.

"What do you mean?"

"Suzanne, if I were in your shoes, I wouldn't be able to keep myself from wondering what Emily had that I didn't."

"I don't look at it that way at all, Grace. Just because Max and I couldn't make it work doesn't mean that he and Emily shouldn't be able to. They are two completely different situations."

"My, aren't we all grown up?" Grace asked me with a grin.

"Maybe it helps that I'm going to marry Jake," I admitted.

"Whenever that happens," she replied.

"Hey, I'm still getting used to being the man's fiancée. There's no rush making me his wife. At the moment, just knowing that he wants to spend the rest of his life with me is enough."

"I get it," she said as we pulled into the city limits of Union Square.

It was time to get going. We were on an accelerated time schedule now, so there was not really a moment to waste in conducting our investigation.

Chapter 9

"So, who should we tackle first?" I asked Grace.

"Well, at least we know where Amanda is supposed to be," she said. "Her repair shop is just two blocks away from Napoli's. Should we pop in on the DeAngelis crowd while we're here?"

"Maybe later," I said. "Remember, we don't have a great deal of time left before we're under the new chief's thumb."

"I'm just saying, we're right here," Grace answered with a smile. "It would be hard to pass up a chance for some wonderful Italian food."

We pulled up in front of the auto repair shop, and I asked, "How should we handle this?"

"We could always say that your Jeep needs some work," Grace replied a little too quickly for my taste as we got out of the vehicle. "That should be easy enough for her to believe."

"What's wrong with my Jeep?"

"Hey, don't be so defensive. I'm just saying that it might be a good way to break the ice with Amanda. I didn't mean to disparage your mode of transportation."

I thought about it and realized that Grace might have a point. After all, my Jeep had seen better days, though thinking that way made me feel a little disloyal. "What should we say is wrong with her?"

"I would think that you'd be able to choose from a variety of ailments," Grace replied.

"Okay, I get it. I'll think of something."

I never got the chance to come up with a cover story, though.

Apparently Amanda already knew all about us, if she was the one striding purposely toward us. "What are you two doing here?" the woman in her early thirties asked as she reached us. "Did you come by my shop to try to pin something on me?"

"I'm sorry, but I don't know what you're talking about," I

told her, caught off-guard for a moment by her confrontational style.

"Spare me. You can drop the innocent act. I've heard enough about you both to know that you're here snooping into something. It's Rick's murder, isn't it?"

"Is there something wrong with us trying to find out who killed the man?" Grace asked her, matching Amanda's tone with equal force. This was turning into a battle before we'd even begun.

"I have an idea. Why don't you let the police do their job?" she asked, clearly disapproving of our efforts to unmask a killer.

"We are," I said, trying my best to adopt a more civil tone of voice, "but that doesn't mean that we can't help out a little. You knew Rick fairly well, didn't you?"

"Who told you that?" she asked me with a frown.

"You have your sources, and we have ours," Grace said smugly before I could reply.

Amanda snorted a little upon hearing that. "Don't bother trying to cover it up. It was that teenybopper of a girlfriend of his, wasn't it?"

"Emma's in her twenties," I said, unsure why it was so important to rush to her defense about her age. "She's hardly a teenybopper."

"She doesn't miss it by much though, does she?" Amanda asked, scoffing.

"Emma might be young, but she was still a threat to you and your feelings toward Rick, wasn't she?" Grace asked her.

Amanda laughed, but it had a hollow ring to it. "A threat? Her? You're delusional."

"You were in love with Rick, weren't you?" Grace asked. "I can see it in your eyes."

Amanda frowned, and I had to wonder if Grace had hit an exposed nerve. "That's really none of your business."

"You can talk to us," I said sympathetically, trying to get the woman to confide in us. I wasn't sure if it could work, but it was worth trying, since we didn't have any real leverage that we could apply. There was no way that we could make her tell us the truth.

It appeared that she was considering it, but then she changed her mind. "You know what? You two aren't as big a threat as I was told you might be. Move along. I'm finished talking to you."

She headed back into the shop, with Grace and me close on her heels.

"Who exactly have you been talking to about us?" I asked her.

Amanda stopped after another step and turned to face us. "On the other side of that door are two men who owe their livelihoods to me. Trust me when I tell you that you don't want to get on their bad sides. When I say I'm finished talking to you, that's exactly what I mean. Do you understand, or are you going to need a little proof?"

"That's fine. We get it," I said, holding my hands up in the air in surrender.

"Good," she said.

At least Grace was staying quiet, something that I was eternally grateful for.

"It was probably just an empty threat," my best friend said once Amanda was back inside on the other side of that door.

"Did you really want to find out one way or the other?" I asked her. "At least this way, we live to fight another day."

"So, we're just giving up on her?" Grace asked, clearly unhappy about that possibility. "She had feelings for Rick, at least that much was clear from her reactions."

"I think so, too, but for now, we need to give her a little time to think about our conversation. The next time that we speak with her, we're going to have to pursue a different line of questioning. In the meantime, we have one more suspect on our list."

"But we don't even know where Denny West is," she protested.

"Maybe not, but we're not without resources ourselves when it comes to Union Square."

"We're going to Napoli's?" Grace asked.

"We are, unless you have any objections."

"Not on your life," she said.

"Then let's go see what Angelica and her daughters might know that we don't."

"Girls! So good to see you," Angelica DeAngelis said as we walked into Napoli's. It always amazed me to see her Italian décor smack dab in the middle of a strip mall. "I trust you are both hungry."

"I could eat," Grace said cheerfully beside me.

"But that's not the main reason that we're here," I said. "We were hoping to have a chat with you about someone in town."

"I'd be happy to, but why not do both, eat and talk?" she asked with a grin. She was an older woman, but her beauty was classic, and it was easy to see where her daughters had all gotten their good looks. "Maria is working the front, but I told her that I would cover for her for a few minutes, so it shouldn't be long. As a matter of fact, here she is now."

A younger version of Angelica came out, and when Maria smiled at us, I immediately felt the intensity of her beauty. "Grace, Suzanne, welcome. Would you like a table for two, or will your young men be joining you this afternoon?"

"It's just the two of them," Angelica said as she gently pushed the menus Maria was offering back to her. "No need to fuss with those. They're coming back to the kitchen with me."

"That's no fair. You get to have all of the fun," Maria said with a smile as Grace and I followed her mother back into the heart of Napoli's. The youngest daughter, Sophia, was frowning over a skillet full of veggies crackling away on the stovetop.

"Turn down the heat a little," Angelica reminded her gently as she reached for the burner's control. "You're looking for crisp, not scorched."

"It's a fine line, though, isn't it?" Sophia asked. "Hey,

ladies. What's up?"

"Pay attention to what you're doing," Angelica softly scolded her daughter.

"Yes, ma'am," Sophia answered with a slight smile, and then, when her mother's head was turned away, she winked at me.

"What can I get you to start?" Angelica asked as we each took a seat at the small table she kept in back.

"Information," I said.

"And some pasta," Grace chimed in.

"Grace," I chided her.

"It's fine, Suzanne," Angelica said as she dished us up two plates of pasta and added a simple sauce to each. As she placed the plates in front of us, she asked, "Now, what can I tell you?"

"Do you happen to know a man named Denny West?" I asked her just before taking my first bite. It was pure bliss on a fork, and I quickly followed up my first taste with another.

Angelica's face clouded a bit. "I'll tell you the same thing I told each and every one of my daughters. I don't approve of you knowing him. He's not a good man."

Sophia glanced over at me, frowned, and then she quickly looked back at the skillet in her care. Did she know something she wasn't sharing? As hard as it was to believe, that's how it felt to me, and it might be worthwhile asking her once her mother was gone.

"We're not socializing with him, Angelica," I said. "He's a suspect in a murder we're investigating."

"Who was killed?" she asked, the concern clear in her expression.

"A man named Rick Hastings," I said.

She frowned again. "I know of him. He's a friend of Denny West's," she said.

"Well, my assistant, Emma Blake, was dating him, against my recommendation, I might add."

Angelica's face softened. "What is it about bad boys that some women find so attractive?"

"My momma used to say that girls dated bad boys, but women were interested in the nice guys," I answered.

"She's a wise woman herself," Angelica said. "How is she, by the way?"

"She's fine."

"Is married life treating her well?"

I smiled. "To tell the truth, I haven't seen her this happy in years," I admitted.

"That's good."

"You know, it wouldn't hurt you to date again, Angelica. You shouldn't let a few bad experiences turn you off on the idea of having someone in your life," Grace said.

Before Angelica could answer, Sophia chimed in. "I've been telling her the same thing for years, but does she listen to me? I don't think so."

"If I need your advice, you'll be the first to know, young lady," Angelica told her daughter, softening it with a gentle pat on her cheek, and then she reached over and turned off the burner. "There. That looks good."

"It should be. It took me long enough to perfect it," Sophia said.

Angelica just laughed. "How sweet that you think you've mastered it, Sophia. Make that dish perfectly ten times in a row with no variations, and then we'll talk."

Turning back to me, Angelica said, "I understand why you're looking into this, but be careful. Denny West is a bad man."

After Grace finished another bite, she asked, "Where might we find him?"

Angelica frowned, and then she said, "He frequents a place on the edge of town. It's a bit run-down, so I'm glad that you're together."

"What's it called?" I asked.

"Murphy's," she said, and then she glanced at the clock behind her. "If you go now, you should be fine, but don't go there after dark. Promise me that much."

"We promise," I said as I pushed my plate away. "Thanks

for the meal."

"Do you call that a meal? It's just a bite."

"What do we owe you?" I asked her, expecting resistance. She had a hard enough time presenting us a bill when we ate in the dining room, but when were in the kitchen, we were treated like family.

"Just your continued friendship," Angelica said.

"You have that without bribing us with food," I replied with a grin.

"But it doesn't hurt," Grace added with a smile of her own.

Maria chose that moment to come into the kitchen. "Momma, one of our customers wants to talk to you out front."

"Is it to complain?" Angelica asked, her features narrowing.

"More like to gush," Maria admitted. "She's dying to meet the woman who made her pasta primavera. She said that it beat anything she ever had the entire time that she lived in New York."

"I don't doubt it for one moment," Angelica said, beaming. She was justifiably proud of her food, and she took every opportunity to enjoy praise about it. "Will you ladies excuse me?"

"Of course. Thanks again for the time, the food, and the advice," I said.

"All free to you, my dear friends," Angelica said as she ducked out front.

Once she was gone, Sophia said quickly, "I don't have much time, but you should know that my mother wasn't kidding about Denny West. He's bad news."

"Are you speaking from personal experience?" I asked.

"No, but Maria went out with him a few times. I'm still not sure what happened, but it ended with Mom threatening him with a cleaver, and that was the last I heard of it."

That was an image I had no problem visualizing. I knew that Angelica was fiercely protective of her girls, and I was proud that she considered Grace and me hers as well.

"What does he look like, so we'll be able to recognize him when we see him?" I asked her.

"He's nice enough looking in a slick kind of way. Light hair, blue eyes; kind of icy, though, if you know what I mean. He always wears a suit and tie, and he puts a white rose in his lapel like he thinks that he's something special. It's kind of cheesy if you ask me, but Maria seemed to like him for awhile there."

"Thanks, we'll be on the lookout for him. By the way, do you happen to know Amanda Moore?" Grace asked as we headed for the back door.

"She's another real winner," Sophia said. "That garage of hers does more than work on cars; I can tell you that much."

"What do you mean?" Grace asked.

"Well, there are rumors that she's running a chop shop on the side at night. Stolen cars come in whole at all hours, but they always leave in pieces."

"Why doesn't someone do something about it?" I asked.

"There are rumors that have been around for years that Amanda has some friends in high places, if you know what I mean," Sophia said with a shrug. "Boy, you two are scraping the bottom of the barrel of Union Square this time. I'm just glad that we're all not like that."

I touched her shoulder lightly. "We never dreamed that you were. Remember, there's darkness in even the brightest corners sometimes," I said.

"Come on, Suzanne. It's time to go when you start spouting fortune cookie observations," Grace said as she nudged me.

"Maybe so," I said with a grin. "I'll see you later, Sophia."

"You can bet on it. I'll probably still be here trying to perfect this dish. Taste this, would you?"

She offered me a bite, and I couldn't refuse. I took a nibble of the veggies, and then I tried to smile.

"It's good," I said.

"Suzanne, don't lie to me."

"There's too much garlic for my taste," I said honestly.

"I knew it. I just hate it when my mother is right."

I laughed. "Don't feel as though you're all alone in that. It happens to the best of us."

"Grace, do you want a taste?" Sophia asked as she offered my friend a bite.

"Thanks, but I think I'll pass. I'm not a big fan of garlic, myself."

"That's okay. You can try my next version."

"I'm already looking forward to it," Grace said as we headed out the back door.

"Suzanne, you need some gum," Grace said as she dug into her purse.

"Is it that bad?"

"Let's just say that you'll be safe from vampires for the foreseeable future," Grace said with a laugh as I took a stick of gum from her and popped it into my mouth.

"What can I say? I took a hit for the team. Now, how do you feel about going to a bar?"

"I'm fine with it as long as I don't have to take a drink. I'm so stuffed I don't think I could swallow a sip of water right now. Not that I'm complaining, mind you."

"We're not going there to drink, Grace. We need to talk to Denny West."

"Then by all means, let's go see if he's in his usual spot and find out what he has to say for himself."

Chapter 10

Murphy's Bar looked like a real dive, but it turned out that we didn't even have to go in. We had just parked when Grace tapped my shoulder and pointed to a man leaning against a brand-new car who was talking loudly on his cellphone. I wasn't sure why she was pointing him out to me at first, and then I saw his trademark rose, and I knew that we had our man.

"How do we do this?" I asked Grace before we got out.

"I say we come right out and confront him," my best friend said. "I have a hunch that dancing around the issue with this guy isn't going to do us any good."

"Why not? After all, we can't do any worse than we did with Amanda."

"Let's go for it," Grace said, and we got out of the Jeep and walked toward Denny.

As we approached, I could hear his end of the cellphone conversation. "All I'm saying is that I'd hate for anything to happen to you."

That sounded ominous enough, and I waited to hear more when he finally noticed us approaching him instead of the door to the bar. "We'll talk later. I said later," he repeated, and then he put his cellphone away. "Is there something I can do for you ladies?" he asked. His demeanor had an oily charm to it, and I could see how some women might find him attractive. I didn't mean me, but some women. His eyes were pure, cold, and terrifying.

"We need to talk, Denny," I said firmly, trying to show confidence that I didn't feel at the moment. "You are Denny West, aren't you?"

He looked intently at me for a few seconds, and then at Grace, before he spoke again. "Do I know either one of you?"

"I very much doubt it, since we don't run in the same circles," Grace replied. "We're here about Rick Hastings."

"What about him?" Denny asked, not giving anything away with his question.

"There's no use pretending that you didn't know him," I said. "The real question is, did you kill him?" I was taking a chance pushing him like that, but what choice did I have? Grace and I had no way to compel the man to talk to us, and if he had anything to hide, I doubted that it would come out in our conversation unless he got angry and sloppy. I knew that it was dangerous poking him like that, but I didn't have the slightest idea about what else we could do.

I wasn't sure what kind of reaction I was expecting, but laughter wasn't one of them. He chuckled slightly before he said, "I'll say this; you get a point for attitude."

"Thanks, but I'd rather have an answer to my question," I said, fighting down my panic and trying my best to smile, instead.

Denny studied me for another moment before he answered. The man seemed to weigh everything he said and did before he acted, and I had to wonder if it was a habit he'd picked up in his line of work. "Fair enough. No, I'm not the one who killed him. Why would I do that, when he still owed me five grand from our last business transaction? Now I'll never see that money again, and you can ask anybody. I hate to lose, period, especially when it comes to cash."

"Can you prove that you *didn't* kill him?" Grace asked him.

I could swear that he was about to answer her when the door of the bar opened and Amanda Moore, of all the people in the world, walked out. "Sorry, it took me longer than I thought it would to set her straight," she told Denny, and then she noticed us for the first time. "Are you kidding me? What are you two doing here? Are you actually following me around Union Square?"

"As a matter of fact, they came by to speak with me," Denny said, "but we're finished."

"Do you two have a death wish or something?" Amanda asked us as she walked past us and slid into the passenger seat of the car Denny had been leaning against.

"No, not even a little bit," I said, which was the plain and unvarnished truth.

"You could have fooled me, because you're sure acting like it," she snapped.

Denny moved around to the driver's side door, but he paused a moment before he got in. "I don't want to see either one of you again, and if you'd like some free advice, I'd leave Amanda alone, too if I were you. There's nothing but trouble if you pursue this any further."

"Now what fun would it be if we just gave up every time someone asked us to?" Grace asked him.

"If you keep it up, *nobody's* going to be having fun; you can take my word for that."

Denny got into the car and drove away, and I noticed Amanda ignoring us as they pulled out.

"Wow, you can actually feel the love in the air, can't you?" Grace asked me after we were standing there alone.

"These aren't our usual brand of suspects, are they?" I asked as we headed back to the Jeep. "Grace, I hate to admit this, but I think we might just be out of our league on this one."

"We're not going to let a couple of goons scare us off, are we?" Grace asked, clearly unhappy about my observation.

"Think about it. We have until tomorrow morning at eight until we have to drop this altogether. Do you want to spend the rest of our time trying to get those two to talk to us again?"

"No, you're right about that," Grace said as I started driving back to April Springs. "When you look at it that way, there's not much about this investigation that I do like. The fact that we can't see it through is really starting to bother me. Do you think this cop Tyler is really going to try to stop us from digging into Rick's murder? What can he do, lock us up? I don't believe that he'd have the nerve to do that, no matter what he said to you earlier."

"Why wouldn't he?" I asked. "Chief Martin has threatened to do it enough over the years."

"Maybe, but we always knew that he was just bluffing."

"Take it from me. I don't think this new police chief is much of a bluffer."

We both considered that for a few moments, and then Grace said, "Well, at least we've still got Travis and Kyle. Neither one of them is a thug."

"Not on the surface, at any rate," I said.

"Suzanne, you sound as though you're ready to give up," Grace replied.

"It's not that at all. It's just that I promised Emma that I'd dig into this, and I'm not going to break that promise lightly. I'm just not sure what we should do next."

"You could always ask Jake for advice," she said.

"I could, but he's got his hands full as it is. I don't want to add any more to his current load than he already has."

"Then where does that leave us? Are we back to square one?"

"I wouldn't say that. At least we have four viable suspects, and nothing that we heard today changes my mind about any of them," I answered.

"Time's a-ticking though, Suzanne. Should we take another run at our two April Springs suspects while we have the opportunity?"

I was about to answer when my cellphone rang.

It was Jake, and all thoughts of furthering our investigation at the moment died.

"Hey, I didn't expect to hear from you so soon," I said.

"Well, we got a lucky break and wrapped things up here. The bad guy is in jail, though in this case it was a bad gal. Anyway, I'm happy to report that I'm on my way back to April Springs."

"That's great news," I said. "What's your next assignment going to be? Do you think it will be the last one you have to do for your old boss?"

Jake laughed a moment before he spoke. "He was so happy that we solved this one so quickly that he's decided to let me off the hook for the rest of my notice. He just promised me that he's going to process my paperwork in the morning, but as of this moment, I'm officially through with the state police."

"How do you feel about it, now that it's a reality?" I asked him gently.

"The honest truth is that I'm so happy I can barely stand it. The real question is, why aren't you, Suzanne?" he asked. There was a shade of hurt in his voice, and it killed me knowing that it was because of me.

I took a deep breath, and then I voiced a concern I'd been nurturing since Jake had first threatened to quit his job. "I just want to be sure that you don't regret the decision later."

"It's not going to happen, Suzanne; you can take my word for it. I don't look back, only forward, and I've got the entire world ahead of me now."

"Then I'm thrilled for you," I said. "I'm just sorry that George couldn't wait another day before he named a new chief of police around here."

"He could have waited for a month and my answer wouldn't have been any different," Jake explained. "I don't know what my near future holds. Actually, that's the beauty of it."

I had a sudden, crazy thought, and before I talked myself out of it, I said, "You know, you could always help Grace and me with the case we're working on."

I glanced over at my friend to see how she was reacting to my offer and saw her simply shrug. What did that mean? I'd have to deal with that after I got off the phone.

"Suzanne, what makes you think for one moment that I want to dive back into another murder investigation, especially working on the other side of the badge this time?"

"Maybe it will be a breath of fresh air seeing things from our perspective," I offered.

"I don't see how," Jake replied. "What other reasons can you come up with?"

"How about because I'm asking you nicely for your help? Does that change your mind?"

There was a long pause, but I knew better than to interrupt it. Jake was thinking, and if I spoke before he was ready to express his opinion, I knew that I'd blow any chance of getting him to help us.

After a few moments, he finally said, "Okay. How about this? I'll advise you, but that's *all* that I'm willing to do at this point."

"That's plenty," I said, happy to have Jake in our corner. "We gladly accept your kind offer."

"Is there anything urgent that I need to know about the case right away?" Jake asked. "If not, you can catch me up in the morning."

"That's the thing," I said. "Tomorrow might be too late. The new police chief starts at eight AM tomorrow morning."

Jake whistled softly before he spoke. "That didn't take long, did it?"

"I'm so sorry," I said. "I don't like it, either."

"It sounds as though we need to expedite your investigation if we can," Jake said after a few seconds.

"I couldn't agree with you more," I said. "How exactly do we do that?"

Jake laughed, and then he said, "Let me make a phone call and I'll get back to you."

"Thanks," I said, but it was to dead air. Jake had already disconnected the call.

"You don't mind me asking him to give us a hand, do you?" I asked Grace as I put my phone aside.

"Why would I?" she asked me impishly. "Are you asking if I should be offended that you solicited Jake to help us without discussing it with me first?"

"What can I say? I saw an opportunity, and I took it," I said as we neared April Springs city limits.

"Well, since I've been advising you to do that very thing for years, I could hardly be upset with you, now could I? As a matter of fact, now that your brilliant boyfriend is on the case, you hardly need my help anymore."

Was she hurt by my plea to Jake for advice? I had to fix

this, and quickly. "Grace, we're a team. Jake might pitch in a little, but it's still you and me, kiddo. Nobody's ever going to replace you as my partner in crimesolving; is that clear?"

My best friend looked a little relieved by my declaration, though she tried hard not to show it. "Okay. That sounds good to me. I love working with you, Suzanne."

"Me, too, with you," I said. "As things stand right now, Jake's just going to be acting as our advisor, and nothing more."

"Unless we need him for something a little more direct than that," Grace said. "Let's not rule that possibility out just yet, either."

"Agreed," I replied with a smile. "We should get our notes together so we can present Jake with the complete picture of what we have so far."

We were still trying to organize our thoughts when my cellphone rang.

"We were just talking about you," I told Jake after I answered.

"I hope it was all good things," he said. In a lower voice, he asked, "I didn't think to ask you before, but is Grace okay with me helping you two?"

"She's one hundred percent on board," I said as I winked at her. It was sweet of Jake to worry about offending Grace, and he scored some points with me for asking.

"Well then, I've got good news. We have thirty-six hours now instead of twelve," Jake said.

"How'd you manage that?" I asked.

"I called George, explained that I was going to consult with you two, and he offered to lose Tyler's paperwork for a day so we'd have a little more time to detect. It's not much, but it was all that I could get him to agree to. Stephen's going to like it, at any rate."

"Officer Grant?" I asked, getting Grace's attention immediately, since he was her boyfriend. "Why would he care one way or the other?"

"I thought you knew. He's been the acting chief since three o'clock this afternoon," Jake said. "This will give him a little more experience before Tyler takes over for good."

"He must be thrilled with the bump," I said. Grace kept tapping my arm, clearly asking for an update as to why her boyfriend's name had come up in my conversation, but I wasn't going to make Jake wait while I explained it all to her.

"If I had to guess, I'd say that it's equal portions of elation and sheer terror," Jake said, and I could hear the smile in his voice. I hadn't realized just how tightly he'd been wound until I heard his relief that he was no longer on his old job. The pressure must have been constant and intense, and I was glad that he was finally out of it, once and for all. Our little investigation would be nothing compared to what he'd been dealing with on a daily basis for more years than I cared to consider. "Anyway, I'm making good time, so I should be there around two."

"In the morning?" I asked him.

"If I'm lucky. Should I go to the cottage first, or just come by the donut shop so you can bring me up to speed while you work on tomorrow's donuts?"

"Don't you dare come by Donut Hearts. Your orders are to go straight to the cottage and get some sleep. That's what I plan on doing right now, since you somehow managed to get us an extension. We both need to be at our best tomorrow."

"That sounds like a plan to me," Jake answered. "I'll see you in the morning."

"You'd better. And Jake?"

"Yes?"

"I'm truly thrilled that you're finished with that part of your life, now that I know that you are happy about it as well."

"Thanks, Suzanne, because I plan on spending all of the next part with you."

"Now I can't stop smiling," I said. "I love you."

"I love you, too. Now go get some rest, and we'll tackle this thing tomorrow after you finish up at the donut shop."

"Given the time constraint that we're under, shouldn't I just close my doors tomorrow so we don't waste any precious moments when we could be investigating?" I asked him.

"No, if it were up to me, I'd keep Donut Hearts open. You never know who might come through your door, or what they might have to say about what happened to Rick Hastings."

"Okay then, that's what I'll do."

After I hung up, Grace asked impatiently, "What was all of that chatter about Stephen?"

"Well, it seems that his tenure as interim police chief has been extended," I said.

"I didn't even know that he'd been promoted in the first place," Grace said, clearly a little hurt that he hadn't immediately passed the news on to her.

"Don't be too hard on him," I said. "He's probably got a lot on his plate at the moment."

"I don't doubt it," she said. "Okay, I'll take it easy on him. Suzanne, are we really throwing in the towel tonight?"

I glanced at the clock on the dash and saw that I still had a little less than an hour before my bedtime, one I shared with grade-schoolers everywhere because of my early morning work hours. "I suppose we have a little time left. What did you have in mind?"

"I was wondering if we shouldn't talk to Emma herself," Grace said softly, clearly bracing herself for my response.

My first reaction was to say no, but after a moment or two of further consideration, I decided that it was as good an avenue to pursue as any. "I'm all on board, but let me call Sharon first and see what she thinks."

Grace smiled as I dialed Emma's mother's number.

I hesitated before I dialed the last digit. "Why are you smiling?"

"What can I say? I just love it when you follow my suggestions."

"I do it all of the time," I said. "Don't I?"

"We're a good team, Suzanne, with just the right balance. I

just hope that nothing changes now that Jake's back." Her smile, for the moment, was gone.

"Nothing has to change," I said. "Think of him as just another asset."

"I'll try," she said. "No go ahead and finish that call."

After punching the last number, I waited for an answer. When she came on the line, I said, "Sharon, is there any chance that Emma would be willing to speak with us about Rick now?"

I could almost hear the frown in Sharon's voice as she answered. "I was afraid you'd call."

"If you think it will be too much for her, we can push it back another day."

"That's not it. You see, Emma has been begging for a chance to speak with you both all afternoon, but I've been refusing her request."

"May I ask why?"

"Suzanne, I know that it might help your investigation, but I'm just concerned with trying to protect my daughter."

"I can respect that," I said, ready to give up.

Sharon surprised me, though, as she added, "I can give you ten minutes with her, if you can get over here right now."

Fortunately we were close. "Don't go anywhere. We'll be right there."

I brought Grace up to speed as I started driving toward Emma's place.

I just hoped that Ray wasn't there.

The last thing I wanted to do was talk to my assistant while her father, the journalist, was hovering nearby.

Chapter 11

Sharon met us at the front door, and it opened before we even had a chance to knock. Instead of inviting us in, she stepped out onto the porch. "Wow, you were telling the truth. That was really quick."

"It was lucky that we were in the vicinity," I said with a slight smile. "How is she doing?"

Sharon looked exasperated as she tried to answer my question. "I don't know what stage of denial she's going through right now. Anger, maybe? She wants whoever did this to her boyfriend caught and prosecuted, or worse. Ladies, please take it easy on her, could you?"

I put a hand on Sharon's shoulder. "I shouldn't have to tell you that I love your daughter almost as much as you do, and I'd never intentionally hurt her. You realize that, don't you?"

"Of course I do," she answered, a little flustered by my frank admission. "Forgive me."

"There's nothing to forgive," I said with my brightest smile. "We all want what's best for Emma. Now, let's go see her. By the way, does your husband happen to be around?"

It was Sharon's turn to smile. "No, he's out chasing down a wild tip he just got from his hotline."

"That call wouldn't have been placed by you, would it?" I asked, grinning in return.

"I have no idea what you're talking about," she said in a disguised voice that I hardly recognized.

"Got it. Sharon, would you like to come in to make sure we don't overstep our bounds with Emma?" I asked her.

"No, I trust you both. Besides, I want her to feel free to speak in front of you, and my presence might make her filter her comments a little."

"Thanks for allowing this," Grace said.

"I should be thanking the two of you. I know for a fact that her boyfriend wasn't much, but he was taken from my daughter before she could see him for what he truly was and dump him by choice. I'm afraid that she might give him more credit than he deserved now that he's dead. Wow, I just heard myself say that, and I'm not very proud of how it must have sounded to you. I'm not evil, and there's no way that I'm happy the man's dead. I'm just sorry for not expressing it better."

"No apologies necessary. We understand how you feel," I said. "Like I promised before, we won't be too long."

"Thanks, I really appreciate that. If you don't mind, I'm going to bundle up and sit out here until you're finished."

Grace and I walked into the house, but Emma wasn't in sight.

"That was intense, wasn't it?" Grace asked in a whisper.

"Maybe, but it's perfectly understandable," I said. "Rick wasn't any mother's dream of the ideal man for her daughter."

"You two don't have to whisper on my account," Emma said as she walked out of the kitchen and joined us in the living room. "I'm not stupid; I know what Rick was. I would have probably gotten around to breaking up with him sooner or later, but I'm furious that I didn't get the chance. He might not have been much of a boyfriend, but he was mine, you know? Does that even make sense?"

I hugged her as I said, "Emma, that's what we're trying to do, make sense of this mess. We've been speaking with your mother outside. I hope that's okay with you."

"I encouraged her to help you, Suzanne. She was never one of Rick's biggest fans, and I don't guess I can blame her. He wasn't always the nicest guy in the world."

"Do you mean to you?" Grace asked softly.

"No, he treated me like a princess, but I saw his dark side at times, too. My mother always told me that we're judged by the company that we keep, and some of his friends were really bad news."

"She happened to share a few names with us earlier," I said.

"Who exactly did she tell you about?" Emma asked.

"Travis Wright, Kyle Creasy, Amanda Moore, and Denny West," I said, naming them all without a moment's hesitation. Emma's insights could be valuable to our investigation, so it was important for her to know what names had made it onto our list of suspects as soon as possible so she could offer her own take on the relationships they'd each had with her late beau.

"Wow, my mother was really paying attention," Emma said with obvious respect. "That about sums up my list of Rick's enemies as well."

"Can you give us anything specific about any one of them?" Grace asked. "Don't filter what you tell us. The slightest thing might be important."

"I'll do what I can. Have you managed to track any of them down yet?" Emma asked me.

"Actually, we've spoken with all four of them, however brief the conversations might have been," I answered.

Emma's expression looked instantly troubled. "Maybe you shouldn't have done that."

"If we're going to find out who killed him, we have to speak with our suspects," Grace said.

"I understand that, but none of them are particularly nice people, though some are worse than others. Would you mind giving me your impressions of them so far?"

I thought about it, and then I decided that it couldn't hurt. "Travis claimed not to know that Rick was even dead, but he told us that your boyfriend was trying to extort money from him over a phony assault case. There's something else, too. Did you know that Kyle had a crush on you?"

"What? No. That can't be true," Emma said haltingly. Was she blushing slightly at that news?

"It's true," Grace said. "He clearly wants you all to himself."

"That doesn't make sense. Kyle has barely said ten words to me in the past six months," Emma said.

"Maybe he's just shy," Grace offered.

"Maybe," Emma said thoughtfully. "Still, that's not enough reason to kill Rick, is it?"

"He also said something about Rick being too nosy for his own good, whatever that might have meant," I offered.

"I don't have any problem believing that someone felt that way about him. Rick was always looking for his next opportunity. I wonder what he secretly might have known about Kyle?"

"We don't know yet," I said, "but we'll do our best to find out. Also, we found Amanda and Denny in Union Square. First, we tackled Amanda, but she just stonewalled us. Then we tracked Denny down, and he claimed that Rick owed him money. He was pretty convincing when he told us that now he'd never get any of the money back, so why would he kill him? The oddest thing we saw all night was that we found Amanda and Denny together by the time we finally managed to track him down. The DeAngelis women warned us that the pair of them weren't all that nice, and it turns out that they were right."

"That's the understatement of the year," Emma said. "If Amanda or Denny had something to do with Rick's murder, you'll never get either one of them to admit it. They just respond to violence, and that's something that you two can't threaten."

"Maybe we can't, but Jake might be able to convince them that it would be in their best interests to share," I said.

"Is Jake actually working with you on the case?" Emma asked, suddenly brightening.

"So far he's just agreed to act as a consultant," I admitted, "but I'm beginning to think that we need him to play a more active role in our investigation. If Grace and I keep working on Travis and Kyle, maybe Jake can shake something loose out of Amanda or Denny."

"I'm still not sure that's a good idea for him to pursue them, even considering his background. Suzanne, maybe it would be better for everyone if you just dropped the investigation before someone else got hurt."

"Is that what you want us to do?" I asked her. It would be hard to just stop, but if that was Emma's desire, how could I say no?

"I don't know," she said haltingly, and then she began to softly cry. "I'm sorry that I'm such a mess. I don't know what's gotten into me."

"If you ask us, you're just about perfect in our books," I said as I hugged her again. "There's nothing wrong with shedding a few tears, even given the circumstances."

Sharon chose that moment to come in. Great. Here her daughter was crying in my arms, and I'd promised to do my best to protect her.

She was about to speak when Grace touched her arm and shook her head slightly. I wasn't positive that Sharon would comply with staying out of it for the moment, but she kept silent and didn't make a move toward her daughter. How long that would last I could not say.

As I pulled away from Emma, I asked her, "Are you okay?"

"Not yet, but I will be," she said after wiping a few tears from her cheeks. "Hi, Mom," she said the moment she spotted her mother. "Thanks for inviting them over. I really appreciate it."

"You're most welcome," Sharon said with a brave smile. "Emma, you look positively worn out. Do you need to rest?"

"Maybe. All of a sudden, I'm flat-out beat."

I knew firsthand that emotional turmoil could take its toll like nothing else in the world could. "We'll leave you both and let you get some rest," I said as I nodded to Grace for our exit.

As we started for the front door, Emma said, "Keep looking for now, but don't take any chances. The second *any* of you feel threatened, shut the investigation down. I can't bear the thought of something happening to one of you because of me."

Once upon a time George had been badly hurt while helping me during one of my investigations, so I knew exactly how she felt. The memory of that incident still haunted me, even though George had made a complete recovery.

"Be careful," Sharon echoed as we walked out.

"Always," I said, giving the mother and daughter my brightest smile.

"Now what should we do?" Grace asked me as we got back into my Jeep.

"I don't know what your plans are, but I need to get some sleep," I said as I stifled a yawn. "Just don't do anything without me," I added a few minutes later when I dropped her off at her place just before reaching my cottage.

"You don't have to worry about me. I'm done sleuthing for the night if you are. I have a pile of paperwork that I have to put a dent in before morning, so I'll be busy until it's time for you to wake up to make donuts again."

"Sorry about pulling you away from your day job," I said, "but I really do appreciate your help."

"You know that I'm happy to do it," she said. "Good night."

"Night," I said, and then I drove up to the empty cottage.

Only it wasn't empty after all.

There was a light on in the living room, one that I knew with complete and utter certainty that I'd turned off that morning.

Clearly someone was inside.

Chapter 12

"Chief, someone's inside my house," I said as soon as I got my stepfather on the phone. I'd forgotten that he wasn't our chief of police anymore, and I'd dialed his cell number out of habit more than anything else.

"You're going to have to start calling me Phillip sooner or later, Suzanne," he said. "I'm not the chief anymore, remember?"

"You seem awfully calm about an intruder being in your stepdaughter's house, whether you're still the chief of police or not," I said, a little agitated by his calm demeanor.

"That's because I know for a fact that it's not an intruder. I dropped your mother off there not ten minutes ago, and I'm due to pick her up again in five more. She baked you another pie, cherry this time, and she wanted to drop it off for you."

"Thanks," I said, feeling the tension leave me.

"You know she's really just checking up on you, don't you?" he asked me.

"Hey, as long as she's bringing me pie, she can do whatever she wants to. I'm surprised that you're so calm about giving something that wonderful up without a fight, though."

"There's no mystery there. She baked one for me, too. By the way, it's delicious."

I got out of the Jeep and walked up onto the porch. "I would be shocked to hear that it was anything but superb," I said as I got out my keys to unlock the front door.

I didn't need to, though.

Momma opened it before I could. "There you are! Suzanne, who are you talking to?"

"Your husband," I said. "Hi, Momma."

"Hello yourself." She gestured for my phone, and I willingly handed it over to her. To her husband she said, "Give me ten minutes, and then swing by and pick me up." Then she hung up before he could respond.

"I hear there's pie," I said as we walked back into the cottage we'd shared for so long together. I took off my jacket and hung it up, happy to have such a snug and cheerful place to call my very own. While the pie hadn't been baked in my oven, I could still smell its delightful aroma wafting its way toward me.

"I thought you might be able to use a treat, especially since Jake's on his way back to April Springs."

"How did you hear about that already?" I asked as I offered her a smile.

"Honestly, men are worse gossips than we women ever dreamed of being. Jake called George, who in turn called Phillip, and he relayed it all to me. So, it appears that your fiancé has joined your little investigative team, hasn't he?"

"Only on an extremely limited basis," I said. "I'm happy to report that he's finished with the state police, once and for all." I frowned a moment before I continued. "Do you know what? It just occurred to me that we are both going to have retired law enforcement officers in our lives very soon."

"Three, if you count our friendships with George," she said. "Don't forget, he's a retired officer as well."

"Maybe so, but he's the mayor now, so he doesn't count."

"Don't ever let him hear you say that."

"Aren't you worried about having your new husband underfoot all of the time, Momma?"

"Suzanne, I'd be lying if I said that it hasn't crossed my mind a time or two, but as long as no one is trying to kill my new husband, he can do basically whatever he wants to and I'll be perfectly happy about it. Don't you feel the same way about Jake?"

I shrugged. "Of course I do, but I'm still worried about him getting bored."

"I imagine that he's due for a well-deserved rest, but if he starts to grow stale, I'm sure he'll find something to occupy his time," Momma said. "He strikes me as being an extremely resourceful fellow."

"I must say that you're taking all of this rather calmly."

"Why wouldn't I? I learned a long time ago with your father that wishing and fretting about what a man does never seems to change anything. At this moment in time, frozen as it might be, we're both happy, safe, and healthy. Whatever the next instant brings will be dealt with in its time, and not one second before."

"My mother, the Zen master," I said with a smile.

She frowned for a moment, but then allowed a smile to break free. "I thought you knew. I happen to be a woman of many talents."

"Trust me, I know," I said. I truly enjoyed being in my mother's presence, something I always realized especially so during our brief visits.

Momma glanced at the clock and dusted off her hands as though they were still coated in flour. "Suzanne, I'd better leave. You are going to need your sleep, and I'm sure that we'll speak again tomorrow."

"You can bet on it. Oh, and thank you for the cherry pie."

"You're very welcome," Momma said, and then she surprised me by taking both of my hands in hers. "Suzanne, we might not still see each other every day, or even talk on the phone, but you are always in my thoughts, and in my heart as well."

"You are in mine, too," I said, and then I hugged her fiercely. It never felt odd when I towered over her. Somehow I seemed to shrink in her embrace as she enveloped me with her arms.

After Momma was gone, I was tempted to have a taste of that pie, but in the end I decided that what I really needed was a quick shower and some much-needed sleep.

Besides, I could always have a slice for breakfast in the morning.

Jake hadn't gotten to the cottage by the time I got up, but I hadn't really expected him to be there. I jotted down a quick note welcoming him back and put it near the front door where he'd be sure to find it the first thing. Then it was off to make donuts and see what my day had in store.

"Good morning, Emma. It's so nice having you back where you belong," I said as I greeted my assistant when she walked in the door an hour after I'd arrived at Donut Hearts, per our usual early morning work schedule. "I honestly wasn't expecting to see you today."

"Truthfully, I was going a little stir crazy just sitting around the house," she confessed. "You don't mind, do you?"

I hugged her as I said, "Of course I don't. I'm thrilled to have you."

"Besides," Emma said with the hint of her old smile as she pulled away, "Mom and I both felt guilty about you paying two salaries when only one of us was working."

"I was happy to do it. If that's the only reason you're back, why don't you go on home and come in when you feel up to it?"

"Suzanne, I was just teasing you. Honestly, there's nowhere I'd rather be than right here with you."

"The same goes for me, only double," I said. "I was just about to do my cake donut drop, so you might want to head out and get everything ready out front."

"Gladly," she said, and soon she disappeared up front. I wasn't sure about her being back at work so soon, but she looked a great deal better than she had the night before. Maybe speaking with Grace and me had been somehow cathartic for her. As I dropped a batch of plain old-fashioned cake donut batter into the oil, I marveled at how resilient my assistant seemed to be. I waited the requisite time, going more by experience than my timer, and flipped the donuts with the long wooden skewers I used when one side had completed its cycle. Soon they were all fully cooked, so I pulled the steaming donuts out and put them directly on a drip tray, skipping the glazing step altogether on that batch. Don't get me wrong; I love making fancy donuts. They are fun to create and decorate, but there's also something that satisfies my soul about making plain cake donuts with no embellishments at all.

After I'd finished making all of the cake donuts—plain, flavored, and fancy—I poked my head out of the kitchen and found Emma sitting on one of the couches, staring off into space.

"Hey, are you okay?"

My question startled her. "I'm fine. I was just sitting here thinking about what's been happening lately, and I must have lost track of time."

"Are you up to doing some dishes?" I asked gently.

Emma hopped up with a smile on her face. "Are you kidding? What could be more therapeutic than plunging my arms up to my elbows in warm soapy water? I'm raring to go."

"Then you're in luck, because I've got a stack of dirty dishes waiting for you in the other room."

As Emma washed the first round of pots and pans, I worked on prepping the dough for the yeast donuts, the second part of our baking day. It was like running two completely separate businesses, and I knew that some donut shops had begun to focus on one type or the other, but I knew that I'd never be able to do that to my customer base. I had equal numbers of fans for my cake and my yeast donuts, and as long as matters stood there, I'd keep making both kinds.

Once the giant ball of dough was ready to rest and raise, I turned to Emma and found that she was just finishing up the last bowl I'd given her to clean. "Are you ready for our break?"

"I'll be done here in one second," she said, and I grabbed a portable timer. A moment later, we walked out front together. The front area was dimly lit, and as we made our way out of the shop, I could swear that I saw a figure sitting at the table where we usually took our break together.

Emma started to unlock the door when I said, "Hang on a second," and I flipped the outside light on to see if I'd been right.

Officer Tyler shielded his eyes from the light. "Would you

mind turning that thing off?" he asked.

I did as he requested, and then I turned to Emma before unlocking the door. "Give us a second, would you?"

"Sure," she said. "Who is that?"

"Chief Martin's replacement," I said. "I'll tell you all about it after he's gone."

Emma nodded, and I made my way out the door, being careful to lock it behind me.

"You're up early," I said as I studied our soon-to-be new chief of police. "Or have you even been to bed yet?"

"I could ask you the same question," he said.

"Don't use me as an example. I'm used to these hours, but that doesn't explain what you're doing here."

He hemmed and hawed for a few moments, and then he said, "As a matter of fact, I came to apologize."

"Really? To me? What for?" I asked him, curious about his motivation.

"I realize that I was probably a little bit too hard on you yesterday. I tend to get that way when I'm under stress, but it's no excuse. I've been told that you can offer a valuable perspective to my job, and I was also informed that I shouldn't have just blown you off the way that I did."

"I'm not really sure that there's much of an apology in there anywhere. Did you come here of your own free will, or did someone suggest that you make amends with me? Perhaps the old chief of police, or maybe even the mayor himself?"

I saw Tyler's face cloud up, and I realized that I hadn't been very gracious responding to his apology. Before he could answer, I said, "Forget I just said that. It's early, or late, or however you might want to categorize it. I appreciate you coming by the donut shop to clear the air."

"You're welcome," he said.

"Hey, aren't you supposed to be at your other job today?" I asked him, trying not to offend him with my tone of voice.

"Oh, I'm going to, but I had a little time before work, so I thought that it might be a good idea to speak with you first."

"Would you care for some coffee or maybe even a donut, since you're here?" I asked, offering the only real olive branch that I had in my arsenal.

"Thanks, but I don't like coffee, and I don't eat donuts, either."

I pursed my lips as I studied him. "You're trying awfully hard to get me not to like you, aren't you? Who doesn't like coffee and donuts?"

"I didn't mean any offense by it," he sputtered.

I let him dangle for a second before I added, "Relax, Chief. I'm just having a little fun with you. Not everyone has to like what I sell here, but it's nice that some folks do. I'll see you tomorrow, okay?"

"I'll be here," he said, and then he silently faded into the darkness. The man was stealthy; I had to give him credit for that.

I didn't even have to open the door for Emma. She must have been waiting for Tyler to leave, because the moment he was gone, she unlocked the front door and was joining me. "What did he want? Has there been a development about Rick's murder case?"

I hated to disappoint her, but there was nothing else that I could do. "That wasn't a professional call; it was more of a personal nature."

That got her interest immediately. "Does Jake know that he has a rival?"

"It's not *that* personal," I said with a laugh. "Officer Tyler was a little hard on me yesterday, but to his credit, he came by and apologized."

"So, all is good between you two?" Emma asked.

"I wouldn't go that far. After all, he turned down my offer of free coffee and donuts. He said that he didn't like either one of them."

"You know my philosophy; I don't trust a man who won't taste our donuts or drink our coffee," Emma said rather sternly.

"As much as I appreciate your point of view, not everyone

has to like what we do here."

"Maybe not, but I still think that they should," Emma said. "Is he working on Rick's case today?"

"Actually, there's some good news on that front. Jake actually managed to get us a reprieve of sorts. We've got until tomorrow morning before Officer Tyler officially takes over. Until then, Officer Grant is taking over for the chief."

"Chief Martin is really done, then?" Emma asked me. "I can't imagine him ever doing anything else. I hope that he doesn't have any second thoughts about his decision."

"I don't think that he will. He seemed pretty sure of himself to me," I said.

"I'm really happy that Jake is helping out," Emma said after a few moments. "Not that I don't have all of the faith in the world in you and Grace. I didn't mean any offense by it."

"That's good, because I didn't take any," I answered quickly. "I'm the first person to admit that Grace and I need him for part of our list of suspects. We're pretty good with normal, everyday folks, but some of your former boyfriend's acquaintances are a tad bit too dangerous for our tastes."

"I couldn't agree with you more," Emma said. "I kept asking Rick why he chose to hang out with some of the folks he tended to gravitate toward, but I never got a straight answer out of him. You know, I still can't believe that he's gone, and in front of half the town at that."

"It was a bold move, killing him in front of so many witnesses," I said. "I'm still not sure exactly how the killer managed to do that."

"Maybe whoever did it was invisible," she said.

That idea, as silly as it might have sounded on the face of it, managed to strike a chord with me. "Maybe that's exactly what happened."

"Suzanne, I was just joking."

"Be that as it may, it could very well explain how it happened."

"Now I'm confused," Emma said as the timer went off. "Rats, now I'll never know what your theory is."

I laughed. "Emma, I can tell you inside while we're working on the yeast dough." It felt good being in the warmth of the shop again after sitting outside in the cold. The wooly worms, as well as the almanac, had both predicted a long, cold winter for us, with lots of snow. Even if it meant a dramatic drop in business, I was all for it. The park was so lustrous and satiny with a coat of fresh snow on it that I looked forward to an accumulation of the white stuff each and every year.

That wouldn't be any time soon, though.

Hopefully, before the first snowflake of the season fell, we'd catch our killer.

Chapter 13

"Come on. Don't leave me hanging, Suzanne," Emma said after we were both back in the kitchen. "How could a killer be invisible?"

"Well, that's not entirely what I meant, but it's on the right track. Think back to Spirit Night. What did you see when you were out in the park?"

"Well, a lot of folks were dressed up in school colors and waving their foam fingers around in the air," she said.

"And what else?"

"Nothing much, except a bunch of people were dressed up as ghosts." It took a second for that to sink in, and when it did, she looked at me intently. "Do you think that's how the killer got away with it?"

"What better disguise to hide behind than a full sheet?" I asked. "I recall that it was tough even figuring out if the ghosts were men or women. Any further positive identification than that was impossible."

"Do you think that someone planned Rick's murder all along, or was it just spontaneous?"

"It was probably a little of both, if I'm right," I said as I uncovered the dough and started prepping it for the next step.

"How is that even possible?" Emma asked, ignoring her workload for the moment.

"I believe that the killer was planning the crime all along, saw a way to wear a disguise, and jumped at the opportunity to use a sheet and blend in with the crowd. You said yourself that you were supposed to meet Rick the night he was murdered, but you couldn't find him. What if he was being hidden by a sheet himself?"

"Or maybe he was in the bonfire all along," Emma said soberly.

"I don't think so," I said. "I'm betting that it happened just before the fire chief lit it up. If you hadn't seen Rick's body there, someone else surely would have."

"Why would he hide behind a sheet in the first place, if he knew that I was out in the crowd looking for him?" Emma asked me.

"As hard as it might be for you to hear, that may be the very reason that he did it," I said. "What if he was up to something that he didn't want to be discovered doing, and the killer took advantage of the situation and murdered him in complete anonymity?"

"If that's the case, then we'll probably never find out *who* did it," Emma said, clearly deflated by the prospect.

"Don't be so sure about that. There are a great many folks working to uncover the killer. I've got a great deal of confidence that someone's going to do it."

"I just hope you're right," she said.

If I were being truthful about it, I had to admit that I did, too. I knew that a great many murders went unsolved by professionals, but I had to believe that we had a chance to figure this one out, too, or why else were we even bothering? I couldn't wait to share my insights with Jake and Grace to get their opinions of my scenario. After all, at the very least it might eliminate some of the folks we were looking at as potential killers.

It wasn't to be, though.

Fate would find a way to step in and ruin my plans yet again.

My cellphone rang around ten that morning, and I answered it the second that I saw that it was my best friend. "Hey, what's up, Grace? You're not on your way so soon, are you?" I liked to tease her about coming to the donut shop and helping me work, and she'd even ventured in once to see how we operated, but Emma hadn't liked it, in fear that I was going to replace her. Once I'd assured her that was never going to happen, she'd been pleased enough to have Grace there, but it had been a one-time thing.

"That's the problem. I've got to go to Asheville, so I can't sleuth with you today."

"What happened? Is everything all right?"

"It's fine," she said, clearly annoyed by her current situation. "One of our district managers two levels above me has a sister who recently moved into the area, and my rep was supposed to drop off a gift bag as a way of welcoming her. She somehow managed to foul it up or she just didn't do it, so now I have to handle it myself."

"Is that really part of your job description?"

"No, but it will make my boss happy, and that's all that I care about. I won't be back in town until after six tonight. Is that too late to be of any use to you?"

"Don't worry about it, Grace. It will be fine."

"Suzanne, you aren't thinking of doing anything without me, are you?" Her question was deadly serious, a tone of voice that wasn't typical of Grace.

"We both know that I can't just stop digging," I said after a moment's hesitation. "Hang on one second." I served a customer, made change, and then got back on the line.

It was dead, though.

I called Grace back, but she didn't pick up. I was about to redial her number when a local mother with seven sons came in, all of them clamoring for donuts.

"Beth, why isn't your clan in school?"

She answered me, clearly a little frazzled with her lot. "They all had doctors' appointments, and I promised them that if they were good, I'd get them all a treat before they had to go back."

"We got shots," a little boy about nine proclaimed as he showed off the bandage on his arm.

"You weren't so brave half an hour ago, Milo," one of his older brothers said.

"Was, too! Ask Momma. Go on!"

Beth intervened. "Boys, remember what I said earlier; you are all required to be on your best behavior. Now, if you each want a donut, I suggest that you mind your manners."

At the hint of the threat, the boys settled down

immediately. In fact, the oldest, a young man named Gregory, clapped once, and his brothers lined up behind him in a perfect queue. It even looked as though they were in order from oldest to youngest, but I couldn't swear to it.

"How did you manage that?" I asked Beth, but she was clearly just as surprised as I was.

"Gregory, was this your idea?"

"Actually, it was Milo's," her oldest said with a grin. "He read about it in a book, so we thought we'd give you a laugh. It's funny, isn't it?"

"Truthfully, I think it's delightful. This is going to be a new Meadows routine."

"Momma, we were just having a little fun," one of the boys said. "We weren't serious."

"Too bad," she said with a grin. "Now, tell Suzanne what you'd like. And don't even think about dragging your feet hoping to delay school, either."

It was clear that a few of the older boys had been planning to do something just like that, because I saw a few frowns crease their faces as their mother issued her warning.

After all seven got their donuts, it was Beth's turn.

"What can I get you?"

"I'd better not," she said as she eyed the apple fritters. I knew that she ran her household on a tight budget, but I wasn't about to deprive her of a well-deserved treat after what I'd just witnessed.

"Don't worry. It's on the house," I said warmly.

"Eight donuts? Really? Suzanne, that's too much. I can't let you do that." She said it, but clearly she was overjoyed by the prospect.

I hadn't meant to treat her entire family sans husband, but why not? With a bright smile, I said, "You're not letting me do anything. It's my pleasure."

"In that case, I'll have another," Milo said frankly.

I looked at him and grinned before Beth could reproach him. "Nice try, mister, but it's one per customer, and you've already had yours."

"If they don't have to pay, then why do I have to?" Seth Lancaster asked. He was a grumpy old man if ever there was one. Eighty if he was a day, he had more money than just about anyone else in April Springs, including my own mother.

"Seth, the moment you bring six brothers in here along with your mother, then I'll repeat the offer." I said it with a smile, but to be sure he knew that I was only teasing him, I grabbed a donut hole, one from the batch of chocolate chip donuts he loved so much, and served it to him.

"You're a real sweetheart," Seth said as he eyed the free offering. "If you weren't taken, and I were fifty or sixty years younger, you'd have to watch out for me."

"That's funny, because I'm watching out for you now," I told him with a smile.

Beth reluctantly took the offered fritter, and then she said, "Thank you, Suzanne."

"You're most welcome," I said.

I might not make a ton of money running my own donut shop, but I had fun, and that was really all that counted in the end, wasn't it?

Wasn't it?

Chapter 14

I was still in a good mood from Beth's visit ten minutes later when Grace walked in, clearly worried about the risk of me detecting on my own.

"I thought you had to go to Asheville," I said as I poured her some coffee in a mug.

"I do, but your life is more important to me than my job. If it means getting fired, then I'm willing to accept the consequences."

"Don't be so dramatic, Grace," I told her.

"I prefer to think of it as being realistic," she replied, and then she lowered her voice so that none of my three customers could overhear us. "Suzanne, we both know that this isn't our usual crop of suspects. Two of them might be tame enough, but the other two are trouble on a level that we're not used to dealing with."

"Grace, we've bagged more than our share of murderers in the past, haven't we?"

"We have," she acknowledged.

"And it doesn't get much worse than facing down a cold-blooded killer, does it?"

"You know what I'm saying."

"I do, but that doesn't mean that I'm going to make it any easier on you," I said. "We've dealt with some rough characters before."

"Maybe so, but not without George or someone else backing us up. Suzanne, neither one of us has ever confronted someone alone like we're dealing with now."

She had a point, as much as I didn't enjoy hearing it. "I'm willing to concede your argument, but I can't delay the investigation. We're running out of time."

"Then don't delay it," she said. "Get George to go with you, at least."

"I'm not willing to involve the mayor," I said firmly.

"Suzanne, how did you ever get to be so stubborn?"

"Probably from hanging out with you all of the time," I said with a grin.

She smiled back at me. "Well, I'd be a fool to argue *that* point, wouldn't I? How about Jake? He's at the cottage now."

"How did you know that? Did you see him?"

"Not him, but his beat-up old truck is parked in your driveway," Grace said. "Is that the best he can do for transportation now that he's retired?"

"Jake loves that old truck, but that begs a question. Are you checking up on me, Grace?" I asked her teasingly.

"Not as a general rule, but I thought I saw someone pull in, so on my way over here, I checked on your place. That's the answer. Get him to go with you this afternoon and I'll run my errand with a clear conscience. Otherwise I'm sticking with you, and let the consequences be what they may. Take it or leave it."

"Grace, you know that I don't want to drag him into our investigation any more than I have to," I said. "He deserves a break after what he's been through."

"I've got a hunch that the second he learns that you're planning to interview suspects by yourself, you're not going to have much choice. He's gotten pretty fond of you, or so I've heard, so the man's not going to want you taking any foolish chances."

To be honest, the prospect of doing this level of investigation on my own had been daunting, but I still wasn't sure that it was fair dragging my fiancé into it so soon after he'd left his old job. "Fine. You win. I'll talk to him."

"That's not good enough," Grace said as she stood in front of me. "You either take *someone* with you, or you don't go, no matter what the consequences might be. Suzanne, I need for you to promise me. Emma wouldn't want you to take any unnecessary chances for her sake, and you know it."

"I wouldn't what?" Emma asked as she chose that moment to walk into the kitchen. "Did I just hear my name taken in vain?"

"Grace is just being melodramatic," I said. "There's absolutely nothing to worry about."

Grace raised an eyebrow before she spoke. "I'll let that comment slide, but I stand by what I said before." She looked squarely at Emma as she added, "You don't want anything to happen to your boss, and certainly not because of you. Am I right?"

"Of course you're right," Emma said as she wiped her hands on a dishtowel. "There shouldn't even be any doubt in anybody's mind about that." My assistant looked at me for a moment before she spoke again. "Suzanne, what did you do?"

"Nothing," I said, a little smothered by these overly protective women I happened to love and respect. All I needed for the trifecta was to have my mother walk into the donut shop, and knowing these two, I wouldn't put it past them to call her in for backup, too. "We've just been talking in hypotheticals. I haven't actually done anything alone yet."

"Well, let me go on the record," Emma said firmly. "Don't do anything, for me or anyone else, that might put your life in danger. Do you understand me?"

"Yes, ma'am," I said. "I hear you."

"Good. Well, I'm glad that we cleared that up. Now, what exactly are we talking about?" she asked with a grin.

"She wants to interview our suspects again by herself since I have to go out of town," Grace told her.

"There's no way that you're doing that," Emma said strongly.

"See? She's on my side, too," Grace crowed.

"Besides, why should you go alone when I'm free to go with you?" Emma asked. "This is for my sake. There's no reason that I shouldn't participate as well."

Oh, no.

That was the last thing I wanted to happen. Emma was too close to this, and besides, Grace and I had enough practical experience to stay out of trouble. Well, mostly at least. I looked at Grace as I asked, "Now do you see what you've done?"

"Why shouldn't I help?" Emma asked a little indignantly. "I'm perfectly capable of looking out for myself. Who knows? I might even be a real asset to the investigation if you give me a chance."

I was still trying to figure out how to turn her request down when Jake walked into Donut Hearts. He took one look at our intense faces, and then he tried to slowly back out again.

"Hold it right there, mister," I said with a grin.

"Sorry. I just remembered that I forgot something in my truck. I'll be right back. I promise."

"You're not going anywhere," Grace said as she looped her arm around his. "As a matter of fact, you're just the man we need."

"Why do I have the feeling that I'm not going to like this?" Jake asked a little warily.

"Because you've honed your instincts to a razor-sharp edge over the years," Grace said. "Unfortunately, it's too late now. You're already involved."

Jake sighed a little, and then he said, "Okay, it appears that I don't have any choice in the matter. Just tell me what I'm in for."

Before I could speak, Grace explained, "I can't help Suzanne with our investigation this afternoon, so if you can't go with her, Emma's volunteered her services instead."

It didn't take any more explanation than that for Jake to know that wouldn't be acceptable on several levels, but he still put up a bit of a fight. "Hey, I thought that I was just supposed to be a consultant on this case," he protested.

"Listen to me. You don't have to do this," I said levelly.

"Yes, he does," Grace insisted. "Jake, you're still going to be consulting with us, but look at it this way. Now you'll be able to consult from up close. How does that sound?"

"Like I really don't have much choice," Jake said with his lopsided grin.

"You do, though!" Emma protested. "I'm an adult! I can go with Suzanne!"

"If you do that, then who will run the donut shop for the rest of the day?" I asked her. I hadn't planned on leaving early, but it would make the perfect excuse. "Emma, if you can stay here and take care of things, then Jake and I can get started."

"That's not fair. *Anyone* could run the shop," Emma said.

"I know that I certainly couldn't," Grace volunteered, a sentiment that Jake quickly echoed.

Taking Emma's hands in mine, I said, "This is important to me. Emma, can I trust Donut Hearts with you?"

"Of course you can," she finally agreed, even if it was clear that her acceptance was reluctantly given.

"Perfect," I said as I hugged her. I popped out of my apron before she could change her mind and said, "Come on, Jake. Let's go."

"Lead the way," Jake said.

Once the three of us were on the sidewalk in front of Donut Hearts, I turned back to smile and wave at Emma.

Her answering wave was a little subdued, but she still managed to grin slightly, so I decided to count that as a win and move on.

Turning back to Jake, I said, "Actually, this is perfect. I can bring you up to date on our way to Union Square."

"I'm just sorry that I'm going to miss seeing the great detective at work," Grace said.

"Isn't there somewhere else that you need to be right now?" Jake asked her with a smile.

"You don't have to remind me. I'm on my way," Grace said, and then she hurried to her company car.

After she was gone, Jake said, "She really cares for you, doesn't she? I believe that Grace would have risked losing her job before she'd let you do this alone."

"What can I say? We're sisters from different mothers," I said. "If you really don't want to come with me, I can do this by myself, you know."

"I have no doubt about it," Jake said, "but just for fun, why don't you let me tag along for the day?"

"Okay, but only if you really want to," I said, trying to hide the relief I felt as I said it. I would have interviewed our suspects by myself if I'd been forced to, but I was just as pleased that Jake would be going with me, not just because he was a man and I was a woman, but because he was a seasoned state police investigator, and this case was tough enough to make me realize that I could use all of the help that I could get.

"Now bring me up to speed," Jake said as I drove us to Union Square.

"Well, we've got four suspects on our list, all brought to our attention by Emma's mother, Sharon. She doesn't miss a thing, and she's been watching her daughter closely ever since she started dating Rick Hastings."

"And are you sure that she's a reliable source?" Jake asked me pointedly.

I glanced over at him. "Are you implying that you think Emma's mother lied to me?"

"No. Of course not. I'm just not sure that the victim's girlfriend's mother is the best source of information in a murder case."

"You're kidding, right? As a cop I know that you had access to all kinds of databases and records, but you're playing on my field now. My main source of information is what people tell me."

Jake took some time to think about that, and I respected the silence. I was sure that it would be difficult to look at things from my perspective after his life experiences in law enforcement, but if he was going to be effective as a civilian, he had to know that he couldn't just flash his badge and expect instant cooperation, and the sooner he learned that particular lesson, the better.

After a long period of quiet, Jake finally said, "I can see where you're coming from, but just because I don't carry a badge anymore doesn't mean that I'm without resources of my own."

"Hey, I'm counting on it," I said with a smile. "Now here's where things stand now. Of our four suspects, we have two tough cases and two ordinary folks who might have felt backed into committing murder. It seems that Rick Hastings had his hands in lots of different things, none of them particularly admirable."

After I brought Jake up to date on what I knew about Travis, Kyle, Amanda, and Denny, he grabbed his cellphone and started to dial.

"Who are you calling?"

"I thought I might check in with one of the sources I was speaking about earlier," he said as he finished placing his call. "You don't have any objection to me calling in a favor or two, do you?"

"Only if you're comfortable doing it," I said. "I mean it. I've got mixed emotions about dragging you back into an active murder investigation so soon after you left the state police. The last thing I want to do is make you dig into another homicide before you're ready."

"There's a difference. That was my job; this one's for fun," Jake said as he waited for an answer.

"I don't know that I'd categorize it as fun," I protested.

"Well, we're not getting paid to do it, so how else would you describe it?"

I thought about it for a few seconds, and then I said, "I like to think of what I do as a public service. Besides, this one's for Emma. If we can give her some peace of mind about her late boyfriend, then it's worth more to me than a salary ever could be."

"Agreed," Jake said. "Suzanne, I've still got some contacts. I certainly should, since I just officially left the force yesterday. Why not take advantage of them?"

"Go ahead," I said. "You have my blessing."

"Thanks. Hang on." After Jake's phone call was answered, he spent a few minutes in hushed conversation, and then he hung up.

"That was fast," I noted.

"A friend's going to do me a favor, check out the names on our list, and then get back to me," Jake explained.

"Man, it must be nice to have friends like that," I said with a smile.

"After all my years in law enforcement, I should hope that I've made some contacts over the years. Do you have any theories about how the victim's body ended up in that bonfire?"

"As a matter of fact, I do. I think a ghost did it."

Chapter 15

"You're going to have to explain a little more than that," Jake said when I didn't elaborate.

Once he heard about the ghost costumes the Spirit Night folks were wearing, he nodded. "That makes sense, and it explains a lot, too. That's good detective work, Suzanne."

"Maybe, but it's still just a theory," I said, discounting his praise. After all, didn't he *have* to support me? We were getting married, for land's sake.

"Until I hear something better, that's the scenario that I'm going to go with." He was about to say something else when his phone rang. "I've got to take this. It's my contact."

After twenty seconds, Jake took out the same type of notebook he had always used while he was investigating, and started jotting down notes. Three minutes later, he closed it as he said, "Thanks. I owe you one. Sure, I can do that. Take care." After he put his cellphone away, Jake said, "Well, that just cost me a steak dinner, but it was worth it. Would you like to hear the rundown on our suspects from a police officer's perspective?"

"I'm dying to hear it," I said, instantly sorry for my choice of words.

"Here goes," Jake said as he reopened his notebook and started reading. "This is pretty thorough. I've got something on each of them."

"Seriously? Even Travis and Kyle?" I knew the two local men, at least in passing, but it still surprised me that either of them had ever had a brush with the law.

"You'd be amazed at how many ordinary folks have records," he said.

"Don't keep me in suspense. What did Kyle and Travis do?"

"Well, it appears that Travis has had two Drunk and Disorderly charges against him in the past, both of them dismissed. From the reports I got, it sounds as though Travis is a mean drunk."

"When did those arrests happen?"

Jake studied his notebook before answering. "Eleven and ten years ago, respectively."

"But he hasn't been in trouble since then?"

Jake shook his head. "No, at least not officially."

"So, what I'm hearing is that he couldn't handle his liquor when he was in his early twenties, but he's managed to keep it under control since then. Does that about sum it up?"

"It's probably a fair statement given what I've just told you, but there's more to his story than that," Jake said. "Could you please explain to me why you are suddenly so defensive of this guy? I didn't think you liked him after hearing the way you talked about him earlier."

"I don't, but that's beside the point. It seems to me that once someone has a criminal record, guilty or not, they're saddled with it the rest of their life. Don't you believe that people can change?"

Jake thought about it for a moment before answering, so I knew that he was giving my question serious consideration. That was one of the things that I loved most about him. He took everything I said seriously and worthy of a well-thought-out response. "I believe that people *can* change, but it's not easy," he finally said. "I've seen it happen a few times in the past, but more often than not, it doesn't work out that way. First of all, they have to want to change, and second, they have to work hard at it to make it happen. Most people just aren't willing to put in the time and effort."

"But you admit that, given the right conditions, it can happen," I said.

"Of course it can."

I reached over and patted his leg for a moment. "Thanks. That's all I wanted to hear you say."

"Suzanne, are you just going to ignore my other disclaimers and conditions?" Jake asked me with that characteristic grin of his.

"For the moment."

"Fine. I know better than to argue the point with you."

"Now, there are three other suspects on our list," I said. "What about the rest of the group?"

"Hang on a second. I'm not finished with Travis yet."

"I thought you said that his record for the last ten years has been clean?"

"Just because no one pressed charges doesn't mean that nothing happened," Jake said.

"That sentence barely makes sense. Can you be more specific?" I asked.

"Evidently Travis got into a fight in a bar just two weeks ago. He got whipped pretty good, and from what my source told me, he wasn't very happy about it."

"If he was in a bar fight, why wasn't he arrested?"

"Evidently neither party wanted to press charges, and the bar wasn't exactly dying to have the police intervene, either. Care to guess who the other person in the fight was?"

"I'm thinking that maybe it was Rick Hastings," I said tentatively.

"Ring, ring, ring, give the lady a prize."

"Okay, so maybe Travis isn't capable of changing, but that doesn't mean that other people aren't."

"I just said as much, didn't I?"

"Let's move on then, unless you have something else against Travis."

"No, that was all I was able to get from my source about him." Jake went back to his notebook. "Here's something interesting. I have a hunch that you'll find this one intriguing. Did you know that Kyle Creasy got thrown out of college his freshman year?"

"No, I didn't even know that he went anywhere. What happened?"

"His girlfriend broke up with him, and he reacted pretty badly."

I felt an icy finger run down my spine, knowing that this man had now set his sights on my assistant at Donut Hearts. "Tell me what happened, Jake."

"According to the girl involved, he became obsessed with her. Any guy she talked to was considered a threat, and he didn't take kindly to competition, even if it was only in his head."

"Oh, no," I said without thinking.

"What does that mean?"

"He's got a crush on Emma, and when I told her about it, I got the distinct impression that she might want to pursue it."

"You've got to stop that from happening, Suzanne," Jake said ominously.

"I know that, but I couldn't keep her from going out with Rick Hastings, so my track record isn't very good when it comes to interfering with my assistant's love life. What else do you have?"

Jake flipped to the next page. "Well, the list grows a lot longer when it comes to Denny West and Amanda Moore. Denny has had quite a few brushes with the law in his checkered past, though interestingly enough, he's never been charged with anything more serious than a speeding ticket. He and Rick both appear to operate in the same circles, and there are rumors that they were business competitors. In their line of work, they tend to take that kind of thing rather seriously."

"But no formal arrests?"

"At least not for Denny, who is arguably the dirtiest one of the bunch. Amanda's criminal record is another matter altogether, though."

"What was she charged with, assault as well?" I asked, shuddering a little when I thought about the repair shop manager and her aggressive manner.

"No. She pled guilty to two counts of embezzlement, and served seven months in county lockup."

"How is that significant to our case?" I asked him.

"While she was there, she met a junior member of Happy Bristow's group of thugs. Introductions were made, and upon Amanda's release, she was offered the job of running the shop where she is working now."

"Well, at least she won't steal from *this* employer," I said half-jokingly, trying to lighten the mood.

"If she does, I can pretty much guarantee you that she won't be going back to jail. I've got a hunch that Happy would punish her in a completely different manner, one that's not approved of by local law enforcement."

"What's her connection to Rick, though?" I asked, curious about how this man in Emma's life had wound up with such far-reaching associates. I nearly called them friends, but they were anything but that, apparently.

"It turns out that he and Amanda were high school sweethearts, and when Amanda wanted to rekindle the spark, Rick turned her down in a very public place. She wasn't pleased at all about the snub, and it just happened last week, so chances are the wound is still fresh."

"That's not the way she told it, but then again, why would it surprise me that she avoided the question entirely? I guess she thought it was better to do that than to come right out and lie to me." I whistled softly. "So, let me sum the situation up. First there's Travis, who got in a bar fight with Rick recently and might be looking for revenge. Then we have Kyle, who might have been trying to get rid of the competition for Emma's attention. Amanda is most likely a spurned love interest, and Denny was a serious business competitor. Does that about cover it all?"

"They're quite the stellar group, aren't they?" Jake asked me with a smile.

"Why are you grinning?"

"These are people I can understand, Suzanne," Jake said as he tapped his notebook. "If we apply just the right amount of pressure in exactly the right place, we might be able to get one of them to crack."

"Just remember, you don't have your biggest weapon anymore, Jake. You're not a cop, so you can't force them to talk to you."

"No, but I've got other ways of ensuring their cooperation."

"Care to share some of them with me?" I asked as we

finally pulled up in front of Amanda's garage.

"As soon as I figure them out, I'll let you know," he said. "Now, let's go shake some tree branches and see what falls out."

Jake seemed almost eager to tackle Amanda without his badge, but I wasn't looking forward to it. Without his shield, he was just another citizen asking nosy questions, and none of our suspects were under any compunction to answer. This was all new to Jake, investigating from the other side of his official status, but I knew it all too well, myself.

Still, if he were going to be of much help to Grace and me, he'd learn soon enough.

I just hoped that the process itself wasn't too painful, but at that point, all bets were off.

Chapter 16

The conversation with Amanda was going to have to wait a little longer, though. Jake's cellphone rang, and as he glanced at the caller ID, he said, "Sorry. I have to take this." After he said hello, a frown appeared on his face. From his end, it was quite a cryptic conversation. "Yes. No. Of course. I understand. No worries. Thanks."

When he hung up, I asked him, "What was that all about?"

"That was my source from before," Jake said somberly.

"Is something wrong?"

"Apparently my former boss caught wind of what I was asking my friend to do, so he's cut me off from any more information from the state police. To quote my old boss, he said, 'If he wants to use the resources a cop has, he has to work the job.' I'm afraid that I might have gotten my friend into a little trouble."

"I'm so sorry. I didn't mean for that to happen," I said.

"It's fine," Jake said as he forced a smile. "Unfortunately, it looks as though I'm going to be an amateur sleuth much faster than I expected. From here on out, I can't rely on old friends. I'm going to have to depend on my own detective skills."

"Which are too numerous to even mention," I said, doing my best to reassure him that everything was going to be okay. I knew the transition wasn't going to be without its own pain, but I hadn't expected it to start so quickly. "Are you sure that you still want to do this?"

"More than ever now," he said. "I'm determined to prove that I'm a good investigator, with or without any authority to back it up."

"That's the spirit. Now, how should we approach Amanda?"

"I've been thinking about it, and I believe that we should tell the truth, but selectively."

"That sounds exactly like what I do," I said with a smile.

"See? There's a reason that you've been so successful in the past," Jake said.

I was about to respond when I saw Amanda approaching my Jeep. Had she been watching us from inside, waiting for us to make our first move? I was beginning to wonder if the woman kept one eye on the parking lot at all times, ready for trouble to appear. How else could she have known that we were there? That made me wonder if she thought we'd been playing games when we'd actually been having a conversation about the reality of Jake's new status as an amateur. Maybe we could even use that to our benefit.

"Follow my lead," I said as I got out of the Jeep and started to face Amanda. Jake looked surprised by my request, but to his credit, he nodded in agreement.

"I can't believe that you're back here again after being warned repeatedly not to return," Amanda said as she started to scold me. As she studied Jake, she asked, "Did you actually bring muscle with you this time? You might think that he's big enough and tough enough, but you haven't seen the guys I have in back."

"This is Jake Bishop," I said. "He wants to have a word with you."

She frowned a little at the identification. "The state police inspector?"

"Do you know another Jake Bishop?" I asked her. While I had not technically lied, I also didn't correct her belief that Jake was still on active duty.

Amanda just shrugged, though it was clear that our presence at her shop wasn't making her very happy. "I haven't done anything wrong," she said a little sullenly.

"Do you really expect us to believe that?" Jake asked as he pulled out his notebook and started reciting the list of her past sins.

"You can skip my highlights. I don't need a recap of my life," Amanda said. "What I meant to say was that I didn't kill Rick."

"Come on, Amanda, you can talk to us," I said. "It's

understandable that you were upset when he spurned you. You aren't the first woman to lash out at someone who wouldn't love her back."

Amanda's face grew red, and real anger blossomed there. "I don't know what you're talking about."

It was clearly a lie.

"Where were you the night Rick Hastings was murdered?" Jake asked. He might not still be a cop in any way, shape, or form, but the man had the voice of authority down pat. "If you didn't do it, you shouldn't have any problem providing us with an alibi."

"I was here, with both of my mechanics," she said. "If you don't believe me, then you can ask them."

Jake glanced at the door of the shop, and then he said, "Your posted hours of operation end at five PM. That would have given you plenty of time to make it to April Springs and kill Rick Hastings."

"I was still here," she repeated.

"Even after you were officially closed for the day?" I asked.

"We had a meeting," she supplied, faltering a little before conveying the information.

"What was it about?" I asked.

"That's none of your business. If you don't believe that I was here, then you need to ask my guys."

"Believe me, I will," Jake said. "You should know that if I find out that you've been lying to me, it's not going to end well for you, so I'm going to give you one last chance. Where were you the night Rick Hastings was murdered?"

"I told you," she said, but for the first time, I felt as though there might be a slight crack in her armor.

"Fine, then," Jake said, and then he scribbled down something in his notebook.

"Do you want to talk to my guys?" Amanda asked defensively. "I can get them out here in two seconds."

Jake flipped the book closed. "That won't be necessary. We'll speak again later."

That appeared to agitate her even more. "Why do you have to keep bothering me? I've already told you the truth."

"When I believe you, I'll back off, but not until then," Jake said.

"What do you need, a videotape of our meeting?"

"That would be great. If it were time stamped, that would be even better," Jake replied with a smile.

Amanda started to respond, but instead, she turned and walked back to the shop, clearly shaken by Jake's appearance.

"All in all, that went pretty well," I said after Amanda was gone.

"What are you talking about? Her alibi was clearly phony, and just as obviously would be corroborated by her crew. She didn't tell us anything that we didn't already know."

"You shook her up, Jake. I could see it in her eyes."

"She won't be as easy to rattle once she finds out that I'm no longer on the force," Jake said.

"Then that's just another reason to speak with Denny before the word gets out. Let's go find him."

"Okay by me," he said.

Denny West was back at his old haunt at Murphy's, perched outside as though he were waiting for someone. Was it possible that Amanda had already contacted him and had told him to expect us? Grace and I had seen them leave this place together the day before, so anything was possible. Did that mean that they might have killed him together? Their motives were certainly different, but that didn't mean that they hadn't colluded to achieve the same end. If they had, Rick hadn't stood a chance. I'd never been a big fan of the man, but being knifed in the heart and left in a bonfire was a bit too much even for my taste.

"I've got nothing to say to either one of you, so you might as well get back into your Jeep and drive away," Denny said as we got out.

"Do you know who I am?" Jake asked him suspiciously.

"We haven't been formally introduced, if that's what you're asking, but it's not all that hard to figure out," Denny said. "You're with her, aren't you?"

I smiled a little at the thought that Jake and I were being thought of as being together, even if it was by the criminal element of Union Square.

"Then you know why we're here," Jake said.

"You're wasting your time," Denny replied.

"Then we'll make this quick. Where were you the night that Rick Hastings was murdered?" Jake asked him softly.

"I was here, just like I always am," he said.

"Are there any witnesses that can back that up?" Jake asked.

Denny just shrugged.

"Okay, fine. I just think that it's a little too convenient that your main competitor was murdered while you were somewhere else that can't be confirmed."

Denny looked hard at Jake for a moment, ignoring me completely. "I don't know what you're talking about."

"Sure, I get that," Jake said, and then he took a few steps toward Denny. Jake was a big guy, but he was usually a teddy bear around me. All of that cuteness was gone now. With a glint of steel in his gaze, Jake said, "I'd better not find out that you are lying to me, or we're going to have a problem."

Denny didn't even flinch, though I know that I certainly would have.

After a full five seconds, Jake broke eye contact and turned back to the Jeep.

"See you around, Denny," he said over his shoulder.

"You know where to find me. I'm not going anywhere," our suspect said, so I followed Jake and got back into my Jeep.

Once we drove away, I said, "Wow, that was intense."

"What's that?" Jake asked, his normal disposition back.

"Are you kidding me? I'm talking about the way you stared him down back there. Where'd you learn how to do that?"

"Cops will be cops, and perps will be perps," Jake said. "We can almost smell it on each other. Once you're a cop, it never seems to go away, that awareness that something, or someone, is bad."

"Now that I think about it, George has it, too," I said, remembering how my old friend and former sleuthing ally had acted around criminals.

"There you go, then," Jake said. "Denny was a little tougher than Amanda was."

"He probably has to be," I said. "After all, Amanda has someone watching her back, but Denny's out there on his own."

"At least as far as we know," Jake replied.

"What's that supposed to mean?"

"Nothing. I'm just running some scenarios through my head," Jake said absently.

"Is one of them the possibility of Amanda and Denny killing Rick together?" I asked after a few seconds spent driving back to April Springs.

"It's something that I've considered," he admitted.

"But it's going to be hard to prove," I said.

"Maybe so. I'm hoping we get a break, though. I set something in motion that I hope will pay dividends."

"What's that?"

"It's too soon to say," Jake answered.

"No, sir."

"What?" he asked.

"It was okay for you to be tight-lipped when you were a cop, but we're working together in full cooperation now. There can't be any secrets between us, Jake."

He took a moment to process that, and then finally he grinned in response. "Sorry. Old habits die hard, you know?"

"I understand that it's a tough transition you're trying to make, and it doesn't help matters any that I've dragged you straight into my investigation, but we need to find a way to make this work for both of us."

"Agreed. Before I came by the donut shop, I had a little chat with Stephen Grant."

That news surprised me. "How did that work out, since you don't have any official status now?"

"What can I say? He trusts my instincts, and there's also the fact that I've had his back in the past. Anyway, he asked me for active suggestions about what he could be doing while he's waiting for his new boss to start, and I gave him a few of my ideas."

"There's nothing that's going to get him in trouble with Tyler tomorrow, is there?" I asked.

"It shouldn't, if Tyler is a good cop," Jake replied. "Stephen might be interim chief for just a day, but that doesn't mean that he can't do his job. I respect him for it."

"So, what tips did you give him?"

Jake shrugged. "Nothing that he wouldn't have thought of on his own. I suggested that he talk to the vendors working during Spirit Night, particularly those stationed near the bonfire. Someone might have seen something that they didn't realize was significant at the time."

"I hadn't even thought of doing that," I admitted.

"Hey, you can't think of everything," Jake said with a laugh.

"No, but it reminds me that there was a reason you were so good at what you did."

"I appreciate that, Suzanne," he said.

"What else did you talk with him about?"

"I suggested that he ask around and see if anyone was shooting film of the festivities," Jake said. "For example, Ray Blake might have been taking pictures for his newspaper."

"Chief Martin was already doing that right after the murder," I said, remembering our earlier conversation when he'd still been in charge.

"What can I say? Great minds think alike. Anyway, Stephen is amassing the photos and video now."

"I don't know if anyone's thought of this yet, but he should talk to the photographer at the school newspaper, too," I said. "I remember seeing her taking all kinds of pictures. She even took a few snapshots of the special donuts I was offering that night."

"That's an excellent idea. Let me give him a quick call."

As Jake phoned the acting police chief, I continued to drive us back to April Springs. We had two more suspects on our list, and our game plan needed to be the same for each of them. We needed to move quickly before word got out that Jake no longer had any legal standing.

Once Jake was off the phone, he said, "He didn't think of the school photographer, either. That was nice work, Suzanne."

"You would have thought of it yourself if you'd been there," I said.

"Maybe, maybe not. Stephen's collecting all of the photographs, and he's invited us to come by the station and look at them as soon as we get the chance."

"That might not be such a good idea," I said.

"Why not? Don't you think it could be helpful?"

"I do," I said, "but it won't do him any good if the other deputies see him working so closely with us. Could he meet us at the cottage instead?"

Jake nodded. "Maybe that wouldn't be such a bad idea," he said as he pulled out his cellphone again and called the interim chief back.

"He had an alternate suggestion," Jake said when he was finished with the call.

"Don't tell me. He wants to do it at the donut shop."

"No, but he did suggest Grace's house this evening at six. They have a date tonight, and he's pretty sure that she'd like to see the photos as well. He even offered to pick up a pizza for dinner. Stephen didn't think Grace would be interested in cooking for us."

I grinned. "The man certainly knows his girlfriend," I said.

"Are you okay with that?"

"It's perfect," I said. "Did Stephen happen to share anything else?"

"I'm afraid that he's a little overwhelmed at the moment, and I can't say that I blame him. The first murder I ever handled solo was a nightmare. I spent half the time chasing down red herrings, and the other trying to tell them from the real clues."

"Has he had many of those so far?" I asked.

"Clues? Not many. There's still no sign of the murder weapon, though he's pretty sure from the medical examiner that a long kitchen knife was used. There was no sign of a struggle on the victim, and no real clues around the crime scene. Oh, his crew turned up a pile of things that might be evidence, including a few footprints in the mud near where the body was found, some gum wrappers, a few discarded cheap bedsheets with eyeholes cut out of them, a wad of paper towels with something crimson smeared on them, and a handful of discarded tickets from the quilt raffle."

"Hang on. Go back. Tell me more about those paper towels. They had something red on them? Could it have been blood? Maybe the killer used the paper towels to wipe off the murder weapon before they got rid of it," I said excitedly.

"Sorry. I'd hoped that it would turn out to be something like that as well, but it ended up being nothing but dull red paint someone had mopped up."

That was disappointing, but not all that surprising. After all, clues usually weren't that easy to come by. "We can't forget that we have two other suspects to interview before we meet up with Grace and Officer Grant. Are you up to talking with Travis Wright and Kyle Creasy right now?"

"After the two hard cases we just spoke with, it will be a real pleasure interviewing civilians."

"Don't be so sure about that," I replied. "They can be just as tough to crack as the pros are."

"I understand that, but hopefully we'll be able to shake them up a little. My presence might not have done much to rattle Amanda and Denny, no matter what you thought you saw, but Travis and Kyle might have a harder time just blowing me off. I've been told that I have a presence when I'm interviewing suspects."

"You do," I said. "Just don't lean on them too hard."

Jake grinned. "Suzanne, I'm not a thug. I can tiptoe around with the best of them."

"That's not what I meant," I said. "These folks live in April Springs, and chances are that at least one of them isn't the killer, so that means that we still have to see them at the grocery store and at the park after all of this is over. We don't need to make any more enemies in town than I've already generated on my own."

"Understood," Jake said. "I'll do my best to handle things a little more delicately."

Chapter 17

To our surprise, it appeared that we weren't the only ones interested in talking to Travis Wright. When we got to his place of business, we saw the temp police chief coming out of the construction trailer alone.

He greeted Jake warmly. "I haven't had the chance to shake your hand and congratulate you on your retirement in person," he said.

"I didn't so much retire as I just decided to quit," Jake answered with a grin as he shook Stephen Grant's hand.

"Has she already put you to work?" Stephen asked as he glanced in my direction.

"This is just temporary," Jake said. "How are things going with you so far?"

"Well, I've learned one thing; being the boss isn't exactly what I thought it was going to be," Officer Grant admitted.

"Is it easier, or harder?" I asked him.

"There are more headaches than I ever imagined, that's for sure. I'm not quite sure how Chief Martin managed to put up with me for the past few years."

"I'm sure that you weren't as bad as you think you were," I answered.

"Honestly, I was probably worse," he said with a grin. "I'm going to give the new police chief a lot more respect than I ever gave Chief Martin."

"What brings you here?" Jake asked him, trying his best to keep his voice casual.

"I'm following up on a lead," Officer Grant said, his expression growing a little stern.

"Anything that you might care to share with us?" I asked him.

"Suzanne, that's not appropriate," Jake said to me.

"Why not? I used to ask Chief Martin about his cases all of the time."

"It's okay, Jake," Officer Grant intervened. "I fully realize that we're all working toward the same goal, even if it's going to be temporary." He looked around, and I did as well. No one was watching us, but he was still being cautious. "I don't think I'm out of line telling you this, but I'd still appreciate it if you didn't let anyone know that you heard it from me."

"We won't say a word," I answered hastily, hardly able to wait for some inside information.

"Hang on," Jake told me, and then turned to the acting police chief. "Stephen, don't say anything to us that you wouldn't want your new chief to hear you say. You've got this job until tomorrow, and you don't want to make any grief for yourself that you don't have to. It's just not worth it on our account."

"I appreciate the advice," the temp chief said with a grin, "but since I'm the one in charge right now, I'm going to make an executive decision and tell you something. Like I said, I'd appreciate it if you'd keep it to yourself, but if you feel the need to share it with someone else, that's up to you."

"Can we at least tell Grace?" I asked.

The young officer grinned. "Why do you think I'm so willing to help you? Of course you can tell her." He glanced back at the construction trailer. "You can take Travis off your list of suspects."

"Why is that? Does he have an alibi?" Jake asked.

"Yes, and it's a pretty good one, at that. At the time of the murder, it seems that he was being watched by a team of investigators in Charlotte on a stakeout. Surprise, surprise, Travis has some connections there that are less than stellar. I just found out that a surveillance team spotted him while they were watching a business under investigation for receiving stolen goods."

"He was at a fence's place?" Jake asked with the hint of a grin.

"He was indeed. It seems that Travis was trying to peddle a load of copper piping that didn't belong to him originally to a fence that specializes in questionable construction materials."

"He was fencing some pipe? Seriously? How much could that be worth?" I asked.

When Officer Grant told me, I took a beat before I spoke again. I had no idea there was that kind of money to be made from stolen construction supplies. "Why didn't they arrest him on the spot?" I asked.

"I have no doubt that Travis will get what's coming to him eventually, but they have bigger fish they're going after at the moment."

"How did you happen to find out about this?" Jake asked him. Was my fiancé upset that his contact at the state police department hadn't known about the stakeout, or did he suspect that the omission had been more deliberate?

"I never would have known myself, but I play tennis with a guy from their force sometimes, and when he heard that I was acting chief, he gave me a call. That's why this is strictly hush-hush. He wasn't supposed to tell me, and I'm surely not supposed to be sharing it with you two."

"We won't say a word to anyone," Jake said, and then he offered his hand to seal the promise.

Officer Grant took it, and the two men shook hands on it.

"I'm curious about one thing," I asked. "If you eliminated Travis as a murder suspect, what are you doing here?"

"I promised my friend that I'd look in on him to make sure that he was still around," Officer Grant said. "He told me that Travis was acting kind of skittish, and he wanted to ensure that he stuck around."

"Was he inside?" I asked.

"Oh, yes, and from the look of it, he doesn't have a clue that the good guys know what he's been up to."

"What excuse did you use when you checked in on him?" Jake asked.

Officer Grant grinned. "I told him that his truck had a broken taillight, and that he needed to get it fixed before he took it out on the road again."

"You didn't happen to break it for him, did you?" Jake

inquired.

Grant laughed. "No, this was completely legit. I just used it as an excuse to look around in there."

"That's good police work, Chief," Jake said.

"Officer Grant is fine with me. After all, that's what I'll be again soon enough."

"So, you won't mind giving up your job title tomorrow to someone else?" I asked him.

"Mind? As far as I'm concerned, Tyler is welcome to the headaches. It's not worth the bump in pay as far as I'm concerned. Don't get me wrong. I wouldn't mind being chief in a few years, but right now, I'm not ready for the headaches."

"You'll be there quicker than you know," Jake said. "Thanks for trusting us."

"What are friends for?" Officer Grant said.

"Are we still on for tonight?" I asked him.

"You bet. I'm looking forward to it," he said as his radio squawked, calling his name. After a brief consultation, he said, "Sorry, but I've got to go."

"Is it anything serious?" Jake asked.

"No, but it's still something that I need to handle personally," the acting chief said, and then he left us.

"Well, that helped us out quite a bit, didn't it?" I asked Jake. He didn't answer, and when I glanced over at him, he was scowling. "What's wrong? Are you upset that you didn't know about the alibi?"

"No, that's not it," Jake replied.

"Is it because you're now officially out of the loop when it comes to information?" I asked him delicately.

"Maybe. It's not easy from this side, is it?"

I rubbed his shoulder as we walked back to my Jeep. "I'm sorry. I never should have dragged you into my investigation. You know what? We've done enough for one day. Should we call Grace, cancel our dinner plans, and have a quiet night at the cottage instead with just the two of us?"

"Why would we do that? Stephen's been nice enough to let

us look at some of his evidence. Suzanne, we can't afford to pass that up."

"Jake, we're not committed to investigating this murder any further. If it's going to be a problem, let's just drop it, okay?"

Jake studied me for a moment, and then he said, "I thought you promised Emma that you'd dig into her boyfriend's murder."

"I did, but she'll understand. It's not worth causing us grief."

"Suzanne, you can stop if you want to, but this has gotten personal for me. I need to know what really happened to Rick Hastings, and I plan to find out, with or without you."

"I choose to do it with you, then," I said, trying to offer him a smile. "Don't be upset with me. I'm just looking out for you."

"As much as I appreciate the sentiment, I want to keep digging."

"Then that's exactly what we'll do," I said. "Now let's go find Kyle Creasy."

"That's the spirit," he said, and we went off in search of the landscaper.

Soon enough we found Kyle's landscaping van; just not Kyle. It was parked in the lot in front of the Boxcar Grill again. Did the man ever eat anywhere else? Jake started to mount the steps when I touched his arm lightly. "Hang on a second."

"What are we waiting for, Suzanne? Hey, what do you think you're doing?" he asked me as I put a hand on the back door lever. The van was parked in such a way that I was shielded from view inside the diner, but anybody coming up the sidewalk toward it who happened to glance in my direction would clearly be able to see me.

I just hoped that no one noticed what I was about to do.

"I just want to see if it's locked," I explained.

"You know that anything you find in there is inadmissible

in a court of law without a warrant," Jake said seriously.

"We're private citizens, though," I said. "I know that it's not acceptable if you're a police officer, but we don't have any official standing in this case, remember?"

Jake looked as though he were about to be ill. "I can't help it. This just isn't right."

"I understand your qualms, but we might not have much time. You don't even have to get your hands dirty. Just do me a favor and go up to the restaurant door and act as my lookout."

Jake shook his head. "Just because I don't like it doesn't mean that I'm going to abandon you," my fiancé said resolutely.

"This all may be a fuss about nothing. We don't even know if it's unlocked," I said as I tried the handle.

It opened a little noisily, and I half expected to see Kyle jump out at me from within.

When he didn't, I tried to slow my hammering heart rate, but I didn't have much luck. The blood pounding in my ears was as loud as any marching band.

"Suzanne, you've got thirty seconds, and then we're closing that door. Do you understand?"

"Okay. Whatever you say," I said, without much conviction. I agreed with Jake's desire to hurry, but I also wanted to see what Kyle might be hiding in his truck.

Jake kept his gaze firmly on the front of the diner as I snooped around in back of the van. It was mostly just a ragtag collection of gardening equipment, and there was not much there to attract my attention. I spotted a few faded canvas tarps, but no sheets, unless they'd been tucked under the canvas. I couldn't reach the cloth to check without climbing completely into the back of the van, and even I wasn't that crazy.

My time was nearly up when Jake said softly behind me, "That's it."

"Five more seconds," I said, and then I spotted a battered old toolbox under a couple of beat-up old shovels. What caught my attention was that, though the box itself was clearly old, the lock on it was not. I shifted the shovels to one side and tugged on the lock. It stayed firm, but the hasp it was attached to did not, and it separated from the toolbox in one easy motion. Lifting the lid, I held my breath, but inside, all I found were a few files, an old pruning knife, and a couple of beat-up old pairs of work gloves. I was about to close the toolbox again when I noticed that there was a recessed tray on the top. What might be under that? In the cause of being thorough, I lifted it and peered underneath.

Jackpot.

In the hidden space, I found a dozen photos of Emma, all taken when she was clearly unaware that she was being photographed. There were shots of her coming in and going out of Donut Hearts, leaving her home, and one of her going into the Two Cows and a Moose newsstand. I grabbed my phone and took a quick photo of the collage just as I heard Jake speaking loudly up front.

"You're Kyle Creasy, aren't you?" he bellowed loud enough for me to hear in the back of the van.

Uh oh. I was about to be caught red-handed.

It was time to act fast.

I hurriedly rearranged the photos, jammed the tray back into place, and then I flipped the toolbox shut. I couldn't repair the broken hasp, but I somehow managed to jam it back into place. Hopefully Kyle would assume that he broke it the next time he opened it. Slipping outside, I started to close the van door as gently as I could. Should I lock it before I closed it all of the way? If Kyle suspected me of spying on him, finding the door unlocked might be a dead giveaway. I pushed the rusted button on the handle down, but I wasn't at all sure if it locked, and I couldn't stall any longer as I quietly pushed the door completely shut.

I was about to join Jake when I heard a woman's voice nearby call my name.

"Suzanne Hart, what are you doing?"

She'd almost given me a heart attack.

It was Gabby Williams, and from the way Kyle looked at me from the diner steps, I knew that I'd been busted.

Chapter 18

Maybe I could find a way to fix it, though. "Hey, Gabby. How are you? I was going to join Jake inside when I noticed that the back tire on this van was flat. Do you know who owns it?" I asked as innocently as possible.

"It belongs to Kyle Creasy," she replied. "Can't you see his name printed all over the side of it?" Gabby studied the tire critically before she spoke again. "I don't know what you're talking about. That tire looks fine to me."

Great. Now I had no choice but to continue to try to sell the idea. "Really? I could have sworn it was going flat." I pretended to study the tire myself, counting three seconds under my breath before I spoke again. "You know what? I think you're right. My eyes must be playing tricks on me."

"Of course I'm right. You should probably get your vision checked," Gabby said, and then she walked past me and headed into the diner.

Kyle was on his way coming down the steps toward me, and not even Jake could slow him down. "Suzanne, what are you doing near my van?" he asked in an accusing manner.

"Hey, Kyle," I said brightly, pretending not to be scared that I'd just been caught snooping around his van. "Did you happen to hear what I told Gabby? I thought you had a flat tire, but it must have just been the shadows."

Kyle studied the tire in question carefully himself before he replied, and then, almost as an afterthought, he tried the door handle to the back door.

It was all I could do not to let out a loud sigh when I saw that it was locked! I did my best not to let my relief show as I shrugged. "Do you have a second, Kyle? We'd like to talk to you about Rick Hastings, if you have the time."

"No, thanks," Kyle said as he searched for his van keys. "I've got a job to do over in Union Square, and I'm going to be late as it is."

"Would you like some company?" I asked spontaneously.

"I could always ride over there with you. I have a few errands to run there myself."

I wasn't sure which one of them gave me the more disbelieving look, Kyle or Jake, when I made my offer.

"I don't think so," Kyle replied warily, and then he got into the van and left the parking lot as fast as he could manage it without being airborne.

"You weren't serious about going with him, were you?" Jake asked me when I joined him.

"Of course not. I just wanted to see how he would react to my offer."

"Well, he *might* have left quicker if you'd set his shoes on fire, but that's about the only scenario I can imagine."

"I'm hungry. Are you hungry? Let's grab something to eat."

Jake glanced at his watch. "Suzanne, need I remind you that we're going to be eating pizza with Grace and Chief Grant in an hour?" Jake asked me patiently.

"I wasn't talking about a full meal, but we could have some cake or maybe even some pie. I know you like dessert, so don't try to deny it."

"I wouldn't dream of it," Jake said.

"Then a treat is in order," I said as I started for the door.

"Suzanne, you can have pie, cake, cobbler, or chocolate truffles for all I care, but I want to know what you found in the back of that van before you get one bite of anything to eat."

I grinned at Jake as I started to dig my cellphone out of my pocket.

At least I tried to.

That's when I realized that it was gone.

It must have still been in the back of Kyle's van.

Chapter 19

"Jake, I don't have my phone," I said frantically as I continued to pat my limited number of pockets over and over again.

"Don't worry about it. It's probably still in the Jeep," he said.

"You don't understand. I had it with me in the back of Kyle's van. I took a quick photo, and I must have dropped it in there while I was putting it away."

"Suzanne, that's not good," he said grimly. "If Kyle is the killer, he now knows that you're onto him, and if he's not, he's got grounds to have you arrested for criminal trespass and a host of other things."

"Either way, I need to get that phone back," I said as I started for the Jeep.

"What are you going to do, flag him down?" Jake asked me as he reached out for my keys.

"What choice do I have?" I asked him frantically.

We were still arguing about what to do when Grace drove up and rolled down her window. "Suzanne, why aren't you answering your phone? I've been calling you for the last five minutes."

I felt my heart sink at the news.

Now Kyle knew that I'd been spying on him after all. If my cellphone was indeed in the back of his van, he had to be well aware of its presence by now.

Jake wasn't ready to concede anything yet, though. I saw him reach into his pocket and pull his own phone out. He punched in a number as I asked him, "What are you doing?"

"I have a new theory, so I'm calling you," Jake said as he started walking over to where the van had been parked.

"What good is that going to do?" I asked, but he just held his hand up in the air, silencing me. I wasn't crazy about the gesture, but then I heard it. "Grace already said that she's been trying to reach me without success."

Then faintly, almost in a whisper, I heard my phone ringing. Hurrying across the parking lot, I looked down in the grass near where I'd been standing earlier and I spotted a sight that nearly made me cry.

My phone was lying there on the edge of the pavement, ringing its little heart out.

I'd dodged a bullet, and I knew it.

Grace looked at the happy tears in my eyes as I retrieved my cellphone, brushed it off, and then kissed it. "Did I just miss something?"

"We'll explain over dessert," I said as I kissed Jake's cheek. "You, sir, are a genius."

"Don't give me too much credit," he said, though I noticed that he was smiling.

"Nonsense. All is right in my world again."

"Did you find the killer?" Grace asked me excitedly as we headed for the steps yet again.

"No, but I managed to track down my cellphone," I said.

"I suppose under certain conditions that's almost as good," Grace said skeptically. "Now, what's this about dessert?"

"Come on in and I'll tell you all about it," I said as I locked one arm in hers and the other in Jake's. I'd just narrowly avoided something that could have been a catastrophe, and I felt like celebrating.

Unfortunately, Jake's cellphone rang before we could get in the door.

"You're not on duty any more, or really, ever again. Let it go to voicemail," I urged him.

"This could be important," Jake said. "Go on in, and I'll be right with you."

"Come on, Grace. I know from long experience that there's no use arguing with him."

"I just hope there's enough dessert left over for him after we get finished," she answered with a grin, but it was already lost on Jake, since he was now in the middle of what appeared to be a deep conversation.

"Who do you suppose is calling him?" Grace asked me as she opened the door for me.

"Don't know, and don't care," I answered with a grin. "All I know is that I feel like a piece of peach pie. Or maybe some apple turnover cake, since Momma's been making me pies like crazy lately. That's it. I've made up my mind. Cake it is. Or pie. I do really love pie."

"That's the girl we all know and love," Grace said happily.

"Suzanne, were your ears just burning?" Trish asked me as we approached her position up front at the cash register.

"No, why? Is someone taking my name in vain again?"

"It's not that," Trish said in a softer voice. "Emma was just in here, and I was nearly ready to call you."

"What happened?" I asked, my good mood suddenly gone.

"Kyle Creasy, that's what," Trish said with a frown.

"What was he doing, Trish? Was he harassing Emma?" Grace asked her. She was nearly as overprotective of my assistant as I was, and that was saying something.

"No, but that's the odd thing. Emma was in here eating, and then Kyle came in a few seconds later. He got a table close to hers, but he never said a single word to her. He more than made up for that by watching her, though." Trish shivered for a moment before she added, "He really gave me the creeps, and I'm not afraid to admit it."

I couldn't blame her one bit. After what I'd seen in Kyle's toolbox, nothing would surprise me.

At least I didn't think it would.

"Well, as long as he didn't approach her, we're probably okay," I said.

"That's just it. As soon as she was gone, he grabbed her dirty napkins and the straw she'd been using. Don't try to tell me that's nothing to worry about. The man is clearly obsessed with her, and you need to warn her about what he's up to."

I realized that was exactly what I should be doing. When I'd mentioned Kyle's fascination to her earlier, there was a great deal that I hadn't known about the man's level of infatuation that I knew now. "You're right. I'll call her."

"When?" Trish asked pointedly.

"You really are rattled, aren't you?" I asked my friend gently.

"Not many folks know about it, but I had a stalker of my own in high school. The guy seemed harmless enough, at least until I found him in my bedroom in the middle of the night going through my journal."

"What happened?" Grace asked her gently.

"I screamed for my dad, who happened to be downstairs cleaning his shotgun at the time. It wasn't loaded, and he swore afterwards that he hadn't even realized that he'd been holding it in his hands. Anyway, he rushed into my room, and my stalker rushed out. Through the window. From the second floor. He broke his leg in three places, but he still managed to get out of there before my dad could catch up with him."

"Did that teach him to leave you alone?" I asked her.

"Suzanne, you clearly don't know a true stalker's mentality. After he had his leg set, he went to the cops and told them that my dad had threatened to kill him."

I was outraged, but sadly, not all that surprised. "How did I never hear about any of this?"

"It was kept quiet because of who the boy's father was," she said.

"Was your dad actually arrested?" Grace asked her.

"No, Chief Martin knew it was a load of hogwash the second he heard it. He refused to do anything about it, and the boy eventually withdrew the charges."

Wow. I'd known the chief of police for a long time; shoot, I was even his stepdaughter, but I'd had no idea that he'd done that for my friend. He got some real credit in my mind when I heard about it, and just maybe I was starting to see a little of what Momma saw in him.

"Anyway," Trish continued, "you've got to tell Emma that she can't be too careful."

"I'll call her right now," I said.

"I'll grab us a table," Grace said, and then she turned to Trish. "Three slices of your favorite dessert, please. Suzanne is leaning toward either cake or pie, but she's still not sure exactly what she wants, so why don't you surprise us?"

"I'd be honored to join you," Trish said. "Thanks for including me."

"Happy to do it," Grace said as she glanced over at me. I decided it was time to step in and save face for Trish. "You know what? Jake is supposed to be in the area. Why don't I call him and have him join us? We'll make it a party. What do you say?"

"Go ahead and call him, but phone Emma first," Trish said.

I stepped outside and saw that Jake was still in deep conversation with whoever had called him. What was that about? I really wanted to know, but I had a call of my own to make first.

"Emma, are you home yet?"

"I just got back," she said. "What's up, boss? How did you know that I'd just been out?"

I decided to ignore the question. "Did you see Kyle Creasy today?"

"I think he came into the diner while I was there earlier, but I can't be sure."

"He was there, all right. In fact, he grabbed a couple of souvenirs after you left."

"Souvenirs? Like what?" Emma asked, clearly a little unsettled by the thought of it.

"Your napkins and your straw," I said.

"Eww. That's just wrong," Emma answered.

"I couldn't agree with you more." I remembered Trish's story of how her stalker had broken into her house, and I wouldn't put it past Kyle to emulate the act. "Emma, how would you like to come stay with me for a few days at the cottage?"

"Suzanne, what's going on?"

"Let's just say that I'd rather be safe than sorry," I replied. "What do you say? It'll be fun; I promise."

Emma hesitated, and then she asked, "Jake's staying there with you now though, isn't he?"

"He's got the upstairs to himself, but I have the master suite downstairs. You can bunk with me, or I'll take the couch and you can have the suite all to yourself."

"Thanks, but no thanks," Emma answered.

"Listen, I know it's not in your nature to run away like this, but do it for me, would you?"

There was such a long pause on the other end that I worried that she'd forgotten about me altogether when she finally asked, "How about if I stay with Emily instead?"

I doubted that the stalker would even look for her at Emily's place. "Are you sure that she wouldn't mind the company?"

"Are you kidding? She'd love it. It'll be like old times when we used to have slumber parties at each other's houses when we were younger. Let me call her just to be sure, but I'm pretty sure that it will be fine."

"If she can't host you, then you're coming to my place, and I won't take no for an answer."

"Suzanne," she said, letting the last syllable stretch out.

"Emma," I said, repeating the pattern.

"Okay. I'll give her a call right now."

"Good," I said, pleased that she was taking this seriously. "I'll be waiting to hear from you, so call me as soon as you know."

"Sure thing, Mom," Emma said, the smile clear in her voice even though I couldn't see her face.

"I'll take that as a compliment," I said.

"Good, because that's exactly how it was intended. That reminds me. What am I going to tell my folks?"

"You could always tell them the truth about Kyle," I suggested.

"No, thanks. I don't want to give my father an excuse to go after him."

"Would Ray really do that?" I asked her. I knew the newspaperman was relentless at times, but I'd never heard of him resorting to physical violence.

"You'd better believe it," Emma said. "By the time he got finished with Kyle, he'd have no choice but to move away from April Springs."

"That's odd; your dad never struck me as the violent type," I admitted.

Emma laughed. "I didn't mean that he'd physically attack him, though he might if he thought the threat was credible enough."

"Then what were you talking about?"

"Nothing short of a complete character assassination piece in his paper," Emma said proudly.

"Oh. That I can see," I said, relieved that it wasn't a question of violence, though I wasn't sure who could blame him when the threat was to his only child.

"Don't discount the power of the press," Emma said, letting her pride in her father shine through. "Dad is a master at that kind of thing."

"So then, what *are* you going to tell your folks?"

"My first reaction is to keep it from them, but then again, if Kyle is a possible danger, they need to know that, too. Why do things have to be so complicated?"

"I don't know, but sometimes they just are. Remember, call me right back as soon as you speak with Emily."

"Will do."

I hung up and turned to see Jake standing there watching me. "What was that all about?" he asked me. "Did I hear you offer sanctuary to someone at the cottage?"

I grinned at him. "You don't have any problem with that, do you?"

"No, ma'am. I do want to say that I'll stay on the couch, and your refugee can have the upstairs bedroom."

"That's awfully noble of you," I said, and then I kissed the tip of his nose. "You didn't even ask me who it was."

"I didn't need to," he said with a grin. "If you care about

them, then so do I."

"I knew there was a reason that I wanted to marry you," I said, kissing him a great deal more thoroughly this time.

The only thing that broke it up was my cellphone ringing, and I was tempted to let it go to voicemail. Only the thought that it might be Emma made me take it.

"Hey," I said.

"Have you been running?" Emma asked.

"No, why do you ask?"

"You sound out of breath," she replied.

"I was kissing Jake," I admitted, and then I grinned openly at him.

He just laughed in response.

"I hope I didn't break anything up. Get back to it, and we'll talk later."

She was about to hang up! "Emma, what did Emily say?"

"She thought it sounded like a hoot. In fact, we're going to make some costumes for the three guys while I'm there. It sounds like great fun to me." Emily loved dressing the three beloved stuffed animals from her childhood, all still her closest friends, in outlandish costumes.

"What are you going to make?" I asked, sincerely interested in what Cow, Spots, and Moose would show up dressed as next. It wasn't all just in fun, though. I knew for a fact that those three stuffed animals, and speculation about what they might be wearing next, kept Emily's customers steadily visiting her newsstand. My ex-husband, her current beau, Max, had even gotten involved, something that I'd never thought I'd ever live to see. That was how I knew that he truly loved her, and I'd given them my blessing the moment I'd heard that he'd embraced the myth that they were all alive.

"We've got some ideas, but we're still working on them."

"Let me know when you figure them out. Do you have Jake's cellphone number?" I asked her.

"No, but I've got yours. Why do I need his?"

"Put it in your phone just in case," I said, and then I rattled off his number. I looked at Jake as innocently as I could, but he just smiled. I was glad that he approved, but it wasn't a requirement. If I could keep Emma safer just by revealing his number, I'd rent out a billboard on the edge of town and plaster it there if I had to.

"Got it. Thanks for worrying about me," she said.

"It's my absolute pleasure," I replied.

"That's all settled," I told Jake after I disconnected the call. "Emma's going to be staying with Emily Hargraves for the next few days."

"Why is she doing that? What did I miss?" Jake asked.

"That's right, you didn't hear what happened earlier. Apparently Kyle followed Emma into the diner, and when she left, he stole her napkins and her used straw. Trish was really creeped out by it."

"She has reason enough to feel that way," Jake said.

"How did you know about what happened to her?" I asked him, genuinely surprised by his statement.

"Suzanne, I don't have a clue what you're talking about," Jake replied. "But that happens enough that I'm getting used to it. I'm just saying it had to be eerie to watch him collect Emma's garbage. Hey, where's Grace?" he asked as he looked around.

"She already ordered our treats, and Trish is going to join us, too. That means no shoptalk, so tell me one thing before we go in. What was that telephone call about?"

"It's complicated," he said. "Can it wait until after I have my treat?"

The expression on his face told me that this was one battle that I had no interest in winning. "Sure. Just tell me this. Has it got something to do with the case we're working on?"

"It does indeed. We might need to strike Denny West's name off our list as well. As much as I'd love to pin the murder on him, things might not work out that way."

"Why not?" I couldn't imagine the circumstances that would exonerate that hood from murder. Whatever it was, I wanted to hear about it.

"That's what I can't say yet. I just got what might be a hot tip, but then again, it might pan out to be nothing, so I'd rather not say anything until I know more. Is that okay with you?"

"No, but I'll find a way to learn to live with it," I said. I'd already done a great deal to help Jake transition into his new life on my side of criminal investigation, and frankly, I was afraid to push him too much further. When he found out whatever he was waiting to hear, I knew that he'd tell me all about it.

In the meantime, I was going to respect his privacy, and his source, but until I heard something solid and indisputable, Denny West was going to stay right where he belonged, near the top of my suspect list.

"Trish, that was excellent," Jake said as he pushed his plate away.

"I like a man who can appreciate a good slice of cake," Trish said as she gathered the dirty dishes together. "How about another piece, maybe something different?"

"What have you got?" Jake asked, clearly tempted by her offer.

I laughed as I shook my head. "Thanks for the offer, Trish, but I'm afraid that we're all going to have to pass on seconds. After all, we're eating dinner in less than an hour. Hadn't we all better skip another piece of cake right now?"

"I suppose you're right," Jake said with a hangdog expression on his face.

"Suzanne, how can you deny him more when he looks at you like that?" Grace asked me playfully.

Trish piled on. "Come on. One more piece won't hurt anything."

I looked around at my friends, and finally decided that it wasn't a battle worth fighting. "Go ahead, then. I seem to be outnumbered."

"No, that's okay," Jake said as he pulled a twenty from his wallet. "You're right."

Trish looked at him oddly. "Excuse me, but what did you just say?"

"I think he admitted that he was wrong, but that's impossible," Grace added.

"Actually, I never said that I was wrong," Jake clarified. "I just stated that Suzanne was right."

"How are those two things different?" I asked him with a smile.

"I don't know. They just are." He pushed the bill toward Trish. "Keep the change, if there is any left."

"As a matter of fact there's a lot, because I won't have you buying me something in my own diner," Trish said. "Hang on one second and I'll bring you your change."

"Tell you what," Jake said, getting into the spirit of things. "Just start a dessert tab for me. When that's gone, let me know and I'll replenish it."

"I can do that," Trish said with a grin. "Suzanne, do you have a minute before you go?"

"Sure. What's up?"

"Grab a few of those plates and walk up front with me."

I did as she requested, but I knew that she hadn't really been asking for my help. I'd seen her carry a great deal more than we were now transporting in one hand before.

"What's going on?" I asked.

"Did you happen to speak with Emma?"

"She's safe and sound. As a matter of fact, she's staying with—"

"Don't say it." Trish stopped me before I could finish.

"Okay. Sorry."

Trish looked at me for a moment, and then a soft expression crossed her face. "I'm the one who should be apologizing. I'm probably just overreacting based on personal experience."

"You don't have anything to apologize for," I said, and then I hugged her. "I'm glad that you're okay now."

"I'm as fine as silk now," she said after pulling away.

"What was that all about?" Jake asked me softly once we were outside.

"I'll tell you later," I said in just as hushed a tone of voice.

"That's not meant to be payback for me not telling you about my call earlier, is it?" he asked.

"Of course not," I answered.

Jake stopped and stared at me.

"Okay, I can understand why you would think that it might be a possibility, but you're going to have to take my word for it that it's not the case this time," I amended.

"Good," he said, and then he turned to my best friend. "Grace, when does your police chief boyfriend get off work?"

"It's hard to say these days, but judging by the time, I'm guessing that he's picking the pizza up even as we speak. In fact, we'd better hurry, or we're going to make him wait."

"Well, we can't have that," Jake said with a grin.

"How can you be hungry after just having a slice of cake?" I asked him playfully.

"The answer to that is in your question," Jake said. "I only had one slice. Of cake, that is. The pizza is going to be an entirely different story."

"You're one of a kind. You know that, don't you?"

"I should hope so," Jake said, smiling. "One is probably all the world could take."

Chapter 20

"How long have you been here?" Grace asked Officer Grant when we walked up to her front porch. He was there balancing two pizzas in one hand, and he also had a box at his feet. She sidestepped the box and kissed him lightly. I was surprised to see the police officer blush from the attention.

"I just got here," he said as he recovered from the kiss, "but I can't stay more than half an hour. Things are kind of crazy for me right now."

"We're just glad you could make it at all," Jake said. "Thanks for taking the time."

"I'm happy to do it," he said. "Is anybody hungry?"

"I could eat," Jake said with a grin as he took the pizzas from the acting chief.

I leaned down and retrieved the box. "Are these the photos and tapes you were talking about before?"

"It's everything that I've managed to collect so far," he acknowledged. "I'm not sure if we're going to be getting anything else."

"This is perfect," I said. "We can look at these while we eat." The box wasn't as heavy as I'd hoped it would be. "Were you able to make copies for us?" I asked him as Grace unlocked the front door and we all walked inside together.

"Sorry, but I couldn't see any way to do that without arousing suspicion. I'm afraid that I'll have to take these back with me when I leave."

"Then we'd better get started," Jake said. "Are all of the photos printed out, or are some of them still digital?"

"Everything has been printed out, but I also managed to snag three videos of Spirit Night. I downloaded them onto my zip drive, so you can at least make a copy of those. Should we watch them first while we're eating, or start digging through the pictures?"

"I think we should watch the movies first," Grace said. "I'll go get my computer."

"I'll get the plates and napkins," I volunteered.

"And I'll get the sodas," Officer Grant said as he headed off into the kitchen.

"What can I do?" Jake asked.

"You could clean off the coffee table so we can eat there," Grace said.

"I'm on it," Jake answered.

It wasn't long before we each had a slice of pizza and a soda in front of us. Grace had brought out her largest computer and had set it up in front of her television. It was nearly as good as having the images projected on the big screen itself.

"Here's the first one," she said as she tapped a few keys on her computer. A bouncing image appeared onto her screen, and it took me a moment to realize that it was the back of a child's head. The operator zoomed out after a moment and the park became visible in the foreground. As the videographer carried on a show-and-tell with her child, narrating everything that we were seeing on the screen, I kept looking into the background, hoping to spot something that might be a clue. There were lots of painted faces and more than a couple of ghosts in the crowds, but mostly it was a night for families as they took in the sights of Spirit Night.

"Hey, Suzanne, there we are!" Grace cried out as she froze the image on the screen. Sure enough, I could see us both handing out donuts in the background to a couple of ghosts. "Remember how they had to lift their sheets up to eat because they forgot to put in mouth holes?"

"Sure, but what does this have to do with our investigation?" Jake asked.

"I just thought it was cool," Grace said, and then she restarted the video and the two of us quickly vanished.

"This isn't much help, is it?" I asked.

"Hang on a second," Stephen said. "Here's what I want you to see on this one. Grace, can you make this move in slow motion?"

"You bet I can," she said, and after tapping a few more keys, that's exactly what happened.

"What are we looking for?" Jake asked as we all studied the screen.

"Wait for it. You'll know it when you see it. There. Pause it."

When the image froze, I saw the wood piled up for the bonfire. It was still unlit, and from that angle, I didn't see any sign of Rick Hastings' body. "He's not there yet," I said.

"Notice the time in the corner," Stephen said.

"6:46," Jake said.

Stephen nodded. "So, we know that at a quarter to seven, Rick Hastings was still alive."

"If the clock is accurate," Jake replied.

"It is. We checked the camera this afternoon."

"Emma saw the body at 7:05, so that gives us a twenty-minute window," I said.

"How can you be so sure of the exact time?" Stephen asked me.

"I was looking at my watch when I heard her first scream," I admitted.

"Okay, then. That's progress," Stephen said, and then he turned to Grace. "As far as we've been able to tell, there's nothing else on this video. Can you play the next one?"

She did as he asked, and we all watched the tape, this time taken by a high school boy filming a girl who had to be his date for the evening.

"Wow, he's really obsessed with her, isn't he?" Grace asked after ten minutes of solid filming that showed little more than the cute brunette.

"Puppy love can be like that sometimes," I said. "Stephen, why are you showing this one?"

"Fast forward until you see the dunking booth," he said. When it came onto the screen, he said, "Now slow it back down again."

Grace did as directed, and we caught a glimpse of the

bonfire again. "Freeze it right there," Stephen said, and then he put his plate down and approached the monitor. "Here's a better shot of the bonfire."

"I still don't see anything," Grace said. "Anything out of the ordinary, anyway."

"Go forward two frames more," he instructed.

When she paused it again, I could see that there was a man standing alone near the stacked wood of the coming bonfire. He was wearing a sheet just as many of the others were, but at that moment, it was lifted up and we could see him taking a sip of soda from a paper cup.

There was no doubt in my mind that it was Rick, being shown in an image that had been captured sometime in the last few minutes of his life.

"That is almost spooky," I said as I glanced at the corner of the screen. 6:51 was displayed prominently there. "So, now we're down to fourteen minutes. That's a pretty tight window of opportunity. Does the third video show us anything that narrows the time of the murder even further?"

"No, the last one is just general background. I thought it might be good to have it for reference, but we weren't able to find anything significant on it."

"We can look at it later if there's time. What about the high school photographer?" I asked.

"Jake told me about your idea. It was a good one. There was just one problem, though."

"What was that?"

"The guy forgot to put his memory card into his video camera before he got started," Officer Grant said with a shrug.

"So that's a wash," I said.

"Not completely. He took quite a few still shots with another camera, too, and fortunately, most of them came out great."

"Do you have them with you?" I asked.

"They're still in the box," Officer Grant said as he gestured to the collection.

I pushed my plate aside. "I don't know about the rest of you, but I'm going to finish eating later. We don't have much time, and I want to see what else is in there."

Grace and Jake each set their plates aside as well, and we dug into the photographs together.

Officer Grant sheepishly took another bite of pizza, and then he said, "Sorry, but this is the only dinner break that I'm going to get."

"Eat up," I said. "You have our blessing."

"What exactly are we looking for?" Grace asked.

He smiled at her. "Thanks. I've been through all of the photos and I didn't see anything particularly incriminating, but in my defense, I had to do it quickly. I was kind of hoping that you three might see something that I missed."

As I roughly sorted the photos and handed them out to Grace and Jake—keeping a pile for myself—I said, "We should all look for any shot that includes Rick first, and any of our suspects second. If Kyle, Denny, or Amanda are captured anywhere on film, we might have some leverage to pry something else out of them."

I rushed through my stack without success, and then I looked a little closer the next time through. I was about to discard one particular photo when something in one corner caught my eye. "I found Kyle!" I exclaimed, and then, just as quickly, I saw someone else. "He's talking to someone. Is that Rick?"

Officer Grant took the photo from me, and Jake and Grace looked at it as well.

"I'm not sure," Stephen said. "It could be him, but I can't say for sure."

"What time was it taken?" Grace asked.

"I have no idea," Officer Grant said. "There's no time stamp on it. What do you think, Jake?"

"It's hard to say," my fiancé said calmly. "Let's keep looking."

Grace was the next one to get a jackpot. "Here's Amanda," she said as she waved a photo in the air. "It is her, isn't it?"

We each studied the photo, but the woman in question's face was partially obscured by a child's helium balloon. She had a bit of smeared blue and gold paint on her face, but I doubted that it had anything to do with Spirit Night. Was she trying to blend in?

"Here's another one of Kyle," Jake said, holding up a photo triumphantly. "He's wearing makeup this time."

I looked at the photo and saw that the paint on his face was smudged as well. Whoever was doing the face-painting hadn't used anything all that permanent. They weren't the only folks with smudged paint in the photos that I'd seen.

I had a sudden hunch. "Stephen, you told Jake earlier that you found some sheets near where the body was found. Is that right?"

"Among other things," Officer Grant said. "You know how it is when there's a fair or anything else going on in the park. Some people don't think twice about littering when they'd never dream of doing it on a normal day."

"I agree that it's unacceptable behavior. My question is, did you look very closely at those sheets?"

"As a matter of fact, I never even saw them myself. Suzanne, there hasn't been time to do everything I need to do."

"Do me a favor. Call the officer on duty right now that you trust the most, and have him study those sheets carefully."

Officer Grant pulled out his radio without argument, which was a good sign. "What's he supposed to be looking for?"

"Unless I miss my guess, he'll know it when he finds it," I said.

Grace and Jake stayed quiet as Officer Grant made the request, and three minutes later, he had his answer. "How did you know?" he asked as he looked at me.

"Know what?" Grace asked.

"One of the sheets had a slit in it," he said.

"A slit?" I asked.

"Exactly where a knife would go through. There was some blood on the inside of the sheet as well. It had to have been left there when the blade was pulled out of Rick Hastings' chest."

"How about the other sheet?" I asked. "Is there anything on it?"

"Hang on. Let me ask." He looked at me oddly, but he'd just seen enough to know not to question me.

"What are you hoping they find?" Grace asked me.

"Something out of the ordinary," I replied.

"Like what?" Grace asked.

"Unless I miss my guess, there are traces of blue and gold paint on the inside of the other sheet," I said softly.

"You're right on the money again," the police officer confirmed after he got off the radio. "How did you know that we'd find paint smears?"

"It just seemed logical to me. At least one of the people on our list probably wore the makeup originally in order to blend in, and then they donned a sheet—probably already discarded by someone else—killed Rick, and then pulled the sheet off Rick first and then their own sheet and tried to blend back in with the festivities, hoping to get away before anyone noticed the dead body."

"Suzanne, there's only one problem with that. *Two* of our suspects have smudged makeup," Jake said softly.

"It might even be three, for all we know," Grace said. "Remember, we never found any photos of Denny at Spirit Night."

"That's because he wasn't there," Officer Grant said.

"What do you mean?"

"While I was on the radio, we just got confirmation that he was somewhere else when the murder occurred. I was about to tell you all about it, but I wanted to hear your theory about the two sheets first," the police officer said.

"How solid is his alibi?" Jake asked him. I had a hunch that he hated being on the sidelines, but there was nothing that could be done about it at the moment.

"Rock solid," Stephen said.

"Nothing is foolproof. What did he have?"

"Denny was running a red light in Asheville three minutes after the murder," Officer Grant said. "We put out some inquiries about our suspects, and Denny was the only one who came up. They caught him with a red light camera, and there's no mistaking him, or his license plate."

"Then he couldn't have done it," Grace said.

"Not a chance," Officer Grant said.

"That still leaves us with two viable suspects, Kyle Creasy and Amanda Moore," I said. "If I'm being honest, I kind of want it to be Kyle."

"Why's that?" Grace asked.

"I don't like the way he's become fixated on Emma," I said.

"In that case, you're going to really be unhappy about this," Jake said as he showed me the photo he'd found of Kyle.

"I already saw that," I said as I tried to hand it back to him.

"Look who's almost out of the picture right there," Jake said as he pointed to a particular spot.

The young woman was stepping out of the camera's viewpoint, so it was natural that I'd missed her the first time I'd glanced at the photo, but when I took a closer look, I could see without a doubt that it was Emma.

"This guy is a real sociopath," I said.

"Not necessarily," Jake said.

"You're not defending him, are you?"

"Of course not. He's stalking Emma, and that's certainly bad enough, but it doesn't make him a murderer. Don't forget, Amanda had her own reasons to want to see Rick dead."

"Who would have ever believed it?" I asked rhetorically. "Apparently Rick Hastings lived most of his adult life on the shady side of the law, but the reason he was murdered was because of some twisted form of love."

"We still don't know for sure that either one of them did it," Officer Grant said as he started collecting the photos.

I held onto the photo Jake had found. "Can I keep this? I need to show it to Emma so she'll see just how dangerous

Kyle is."

"Sorry, but it's evidence," he said sadly.

"May she at least take a picture of it with her cellphone?" Jake asked.

"I probably shouldn't even allow that," he said, and then the acting police chief winked at me. "Jake, do you have a second? I'd like your advice about something else. It shouldn't take more than thirty seconds."

As he turned away, I didn't need to be hit over the head to get his message. Taking out my cellphone, I snapped three quick pictures of the photo just as Officer Grant turned back to me and grinned as he reached for the photo. "Like I said, I'm sorry that I can't help, but this is official police business."

"I understand," I said with a smile, "and I'll try not to hold it against you."

"I'd appreciate that," he said, and then he collected the photos and the zip drive. "Sorry, but I really do have to run." Officer Grant was heading for the door when he stopped and looked at me. "One more thing. How did you know that we'd find a slit in one of the sheets?"

"I'd love to say that it was directly due to deductive reasoning, but the truth is that I didn't know it would be there at all."

"So then, you got lucky?" he asked me with a smile.

"Hey, I'm never one to discount Lady Fortune when she grins down on me."

He accepted that with a nod, and then continued his progress outside.

Grace walked him out, and the moment they were outside, I told Jake, "Thanks. I don't know why I didn't think to do that myself."

"I'm sure that you would have come up with it on your own," Jake said.

"Probably, but I doubt that I would have done it in time. What do you think?"

"We're making progress," Jake allowed.

"I'm not talking about the case. Well, at least not directly. How does it feel being on this side of the investigation?"

Jake scowled for a moment before answering. "I have to admit that I'm not all that fond of it, but I assume that I'll get used to it over time."

"It will get better. I promise you."

"I think you're right, but in the meantime, it's tough to sit here and just do nothing."

"Jake, it may look like we're not getting results, but so far, our investigation has been phenomenally successful."

"If you say so," he said.

"Was that what your earlier lead was about?" I asked him. "Did you know about the red light camera all along?"

"No, I didn't have a clue. That came out of left field. Maybe that's another reason I'm feeling so frustrated. I'm getting my information second and even third hand. It's no way to run an investigation."

"Sometimes it's the best that we can do, though," I said.

Grace came back in a minute later with a smile on her face. "That was awfully nice of Stephen, wasn't it?"

"Providing the food, or the information?" I asked her.

"Why can't it be both?" she asked in return.

"Truth be told, I'm going to miss him being our chief," I said. "I have a hunch that Chief Tyler isn't going to be nearly as cooperative."

"I thought you two had worked things out?" Grace asked.

"Let's just say that it felt more like we were declaring a truce. How long that will last, I have no idea. In the meantime, let's take advantage of the time that we've got left before he takes over for good."

"The handful of hours we have left, at any rate," Jake said. "We can't forget that tomorrow at eight AM, we all turn back into pumpkins."

"Then we'd better get busy solving this murder, hadn't we?" I asked.

Chapter 21

"So, where do we start?" I asked Jake.

"Let's have one more chat with our final two suspects. I have a feeling that if we push them each a little harder, one of them is going to crack."

"Kyle seems particularly on edge to me," Grace said, "but do you honestly think that Amanda is going to respond to pressure from three civilians?"

Jake grinned. "I'm counting on her still not knowing that I've left the force."

"Are you okay with implying that?" I asked him.

"Suzanne, I agree that it's a gray area, but what other choice do we have? I've never been pulled off of a case before I've found the killer, and I don't want to end things that way."

"So, this has become important to you, too," I said.

"Of course it has. Once you and Grace involved me in it, I started to take the murder personally. That's one of the secrets of my past success. Too many cops become dispassionate over the years and they stop caring on a human level. I never let that happen to me, though I'm the first one to admit that I came close a time or two." Jake must have known how solemn he sounded, because he clapped his hands together once to dispel the sobriety of the mood and added, "Now, who's ready to go find Kyle and Amanda?"

"I am," I said.

"Well, you're certainly not going anywhere without me," Grace added.

"Then let's go."

As we got into my Jeep, Grace in the back and Jake in the passenger seat up front beside me, I started the engine in the growing darkness as night began to fall in earnest. We were at that time of year where we were losing light in the morning and evening at an alarming rate, and the temperature was definitely starting to drop.

"What are we waiting for?" Jake asked as the Jeep idled in Grace's driveway.

"Which one do we tackle first?" I asked. "I have to know where we're going before I can leave."

"Well, Kyle is closer, so I say we go after him first. Do either one of you have any objections to that?" Jake asked as he glanced at me first, and then Grace.

"One is as good as the other in my book," Grace said from the back.

"Kyle's it is, then," I said, and I started driving.

"When we get there, I want you both to let me handle things," Jake said as I made my way to Kyle's place. I knew that he lived in a small guest cottage on the outskirts of town, a small home overgrown and unkempt. It had belonged to a friend of my mother's once, and I'd visited there when it had been in pristine condition, but the last time I'd been by, I'd noticed that it had been severely run-down.

"I thought we were all doing this together, Jake," Grace said.

"We are," he said as he turned slightly to face her. "It's just that I've had experience doing this kind of thing before."

"So have we," Grace protested.

"Hey, take it easy. We're on the same team here," I said.

"I know that, but I don't want Jake to forget that we're all in this together."

"You're right. That didn't come out the way that I'd intended it to. I was wrong, and I apologize," Jake told Grace.

I glanced in my rearview mirror and saw Grace studying Jake before she ever glanced over at me. "Does he do that very often?"

"What, be wrong?" Jake asked.

Grace dismissed that. "No, lots of folks are wrong more than they realize, or are willing to admit. I'm just not used to someone owning up to it and apologizing."

"You've just been hanging around with the wrong kind of people," Jake said with a smile.

"Clearly," she said.

"Okay, then it's settled. We go together, no matter what," I said. "All I've got is a tire iron for defense. Is that going to be enough?"

"Don't worry about it," Jake said.

"What does that mean?" I asked.

"I'm armed."

"You've still got a gun? I figured that they'd make you give it back," I said, surprised that I hadn't known that Jake was still armed. I knew that he had carried a gun as a state police inspector, but I hadn't realized that he owned one personally as well.

"Suzanne, it's perfectly legal for me to carry a weapon. I have a permit and everything. You should know better than anyone that sometimes my past can come back to haunt me. I've put too many people away to go around defenseless."

"I doubt that you're all that vulnerable even without your gun," Grace said with a grin.

"I'm not, but I still feel better having it on me, especially in times like this."

"Where do you keep it?" I asked, now curious about it. "I didn't see a holster."

"What, do you mean like a cowboy?" Grace asked.

"I've got it in a shoulder holster," Jake said as he pulled his jacket back a little.

Sure enough, there it was. How had I missed it before? I prided myself on my observational skills, but I'd somehow failed to see that Jake had been carrying a weapon all along.

As we neared the run-down cottage, I stopped a hundred feet from the door.

"There it is," I said as I turned the engine off.

"Let's go," Jake said as he put his hand on the door. "If it's okay with you two, I'd like to try to intimidate him a little."

"What are you going to do, kick the front door in?" Grace asked with a smile.

"Not a chance, but I am going to see how far I can push him using just words," Jake answered.

"This ought to be good," I said.

At that moment, Grace's cellphone rang. "It's Stephen," she said. "Do you mind if I take it?"

"No, go ahead," Jake answered. "It could be important."

After a moment of conversation, I heard Grace say, "You guys go on. I need to take this."

"Is it about the murder case?" I asked her.

"No, it's more like a crisis of faith. Apparently he feels overwhelmed by everything, and he needs a little pep talk."

"Then he came to the right gal," I said with a smile.

"I'd like to think so," Grace replied.

"We can wait here if you want to be a part of this," Jake said.

"Thanks, but I really need some privacy to do this properly. Go on. I'll be fine."

"If you're sure," Jake said, and then he turned to me. "Are you ready?"

"I'm raring to go," I said.

"Then let's do this."

As we approached Kyle's front door, I saw Jake pull out his handgun and keep it at his side.

"Do you honestly think that you're going to need that?" I asked him.

"Probably not, but I'd like to have it out and ready, just in case. Is that okay with you?"

"It makes me feel a little safer, in all honesty."

"Well, don't let up just because I'm armed," Jake said. "A weapon is just a tool. I'd like to think that I don't have to rely on it to do my job."

I didn't want to be the one to remind him that he didn't hold that particular position anymore, so I just nodded in the last remnants of daylight. Dusk was ending, and very soon we would be in darkness. That was going to add a whole new layer of complications to our task at hand, but I refused to worry about it, since there was nothing that I could do to stop it from coming.

Jake and I got to the front door, and I could see a light on somewhere inside. At first I thought that more than one person was inside when I heard the whispers of a conversation filtering through to us, but then I realized that a television was playing in the background, barely loud enough for us to hear.

"Kyle, this is Jake Bishop! I need to speak with you!" Jake commanded after banging hard on the front door three times with the flat part of his hand. His voice was even more intimidating than his knock, and I was glad that I wasn't on the other side of that door.

There was no answer.

"Kyle, you don't want me coming in there after you!" Jake boomed.

I heard something fall over inside just then, and I braced myself for a confrontation.

Instead, I suddenly heard the back door slam shut.

Kyle had been in there, but now he was running away.

"Stay here!" Jake barked at me as he started around back in the growing darkness.

"Not a chance," I answered as I followed him. If something was about to happen, I meant to be a part of it.

Jake just shrugged and moved on. He was in full attack mode now, and it was a scary sight.

As we rushed around the house, Jake shouted again. "You can't run forever. Stand your ground and face me like a man!"

I listened for a response, but I didn't hear a word of reply.

In fact, I couldn't even hear anyone ahead of us.

"Where did he go?"

Jake held up a hand, and we both stopped and listened.

There wasn't a sound anywhere around but crickets chirping.

"We lost him," Jake said softly, though I noticed that he still kept his gun by his side.

"Well, we certainly managed to get his attention. What do we do now?"

Jake shrugged. "There's really not much that we can do

here. Besides, I'm not in the mood to stand around and wait for him to show up again. At the very least, we've given him something to think about. Now let's go find Amanda Moore and see if we can rattle her up a little, too."

"I'm guessing that it won't be as easy to do as it was with Kyle," I said as we walked back to my Jeep.

"You never know. I have my ways," Jake said, and I could barely make out his grin in the last vestiges of light for the day.

"I never doubted it for a second," I said.

Grace was still on the phone when we got back, but she ended the conversation as soon as I closed my door.

"How did your conversation go?" I asked her.

"He's fine. There's no doubt in my mind that he'll rise to the occasion. What was all the yelling about?"

Jake laughed. "That wasn't yelling. I was merely announcing our presence on the scene."

Grace grinned. "Well done, then, because it nearly scared the pants off me, and I was all the way out here. What did Kyle have to say for himself?"

"We never got a chance to find out. He ran like a scared little rabbit," I replied.

"That's pretty telling right there, isn't it? Do we go after him in the dark?" It was clear that she didn't relish the prospect of stumbling around in the darkness, and for that matter, neither did I.

"Without a search party, we'd probably never be able to track him down," Jake said. "I say we go talk to Amanda again."

"If you're as forceful with her as you were with Kyle, you might just end the night with two confessions before the night is over," I said.

"Actually, one is all we need," Jake said.

It was Jake's cellphone's turn to ring as I pulled away from the cottage.

"Hey. Okay. Hang on. Give me one second." Jake covered the phone as he explained, "It's my friend from the force, Terry Hanlan. I told him that he could call me when he got the chance. He needs some advice about a case he's working on. Do you mind?"

I knew State Police Inspector Hanlan pretty well myself. He'd been the one who'd first told me that Jake had been shot in the line of duty, and he'd become a friend of mine over time, as well as being Jake's. "Go on. Tell him I said hello."

Jake did as I requested, and then he got so involved with the conversation that he might as well not have been with us on the drive to Union Square.

As I drove, I asked Grace softly, "Is Stephen really okay?"

"He's fine."

"I'll bet he's glad that he won't be the police chief in the morning," I offered.

"On the contrary. It turns out that now he's sorry to be giving it up. That's why he called me. He wanted my opinion on why George didn't choose him as chief, instead of bringing someone else in from the outside."

"What did you tell him?" I asked.

"Well, I tried to explain that if he'd only had more experience, he would have been the logical choice, since he's certainly good enough at what he does. He wanted to know if I thought that his age was a factor, and I told him that it probably played a part in the decision, too."

"How did that go over?" I asked. I knew that Officer Grant was a little sensitive about the fact that he was younger than Grace, and having it be an issue in his job as well couldn't help matters between them.

"He said that he understood, but I'm still not sure. Anyway, I managed to convince him that no matter how brief it's been, his time as interim police chief has been a good thing."

"How did you manage to do that?" I asked, once again in awe of my friend's ability to handle delicate situations.

"I told him that if nothing else, it would look great on his resume," I said.

"And that actually helped?"

"Who knows? It got him laughing, and that was really all that I was after." Grace looked out the window, and then she turned back to face me as I glanced at her in the rearview mirror. "Suzanne, how do we keep managing to get ourselves into these situations?"

"We care about the people around us," I said after giving it some thought. "Can we help it if most of them are prone to getting into trouble?"

Grace laughed. "I don't suppose we can."

Jake wrapped up his telephone conversation, and after he put his cellphone away, he asked, "What have you two been talking about?"

"Life, the weather, and the crescent moon," I said lightly, not wanting to reveal what Grace had just told me. "How's Terry doing?"

"To be honest with you, right now he's baffled. He sends his love, by the way."

"Is it a tough case?"

"It sounds like it," Jake said after a moment of hesitation.

"Is that a wistful note I hear in your voice?" I asked him.

"What? No. I just wish that I could help him, but without seeing all of the evidence for myself, there's not much that I can do for him."

"It's still nice that you're willing to lend a hand even after you're gone," I said as I patted his leg gently.

"You know as well as I do that Terry's been there for me in the past. I'll help him in whatever way I can," Jake said.

"You miss it a little, don't you?" Grace asked softly from the back. "Go on, you can admit it to us."

"I miss some of the people, but if the bad guys didn't end up killing me, then the stress probably would have. No, I'm ready to see what a calm, ordinary life is all about."

"I hate to break it to you," Grace said, "but if that's what you're looking for, then you're probably marrying the wrong girl."

"Hey," I said in jest. "You're not helping."

"What can I say? Is it true, or not?" she asked playfully.

"I refuse to answer on the grounds that I might incriminate myself," I answered with a smile.

Jake grinned at me. "Don't worry, Suzanne. It turns out that you bring just the right amount of crazy to my life."

"Thanks. I think."

"It was a compliment, I assure you," Jake said.

We were in Union Square now, approaching the garage where Amanda worked. "I just realized that I don't know where she lives," I said.

"It doesn't matter. There are three cars out front, and all of the lights inside are still on." Jake suddenly barked out to me, "Pull over and kill your lights!"

I did as I was told without question.

Once I was parked, I whispered, "What's going on?"

"You don't have to whisper. I doubt they can hear us from all the way over here. Look."

I glanced over at the garage and saw that the front door had been cracked a bit earlier, but now it was beginning to open fully. How had Jake spotted that from so far away in the darkness? The man could teach me a few things about observation, that was for sure.

Two large and husky men were leaving the garage, but before they left, they were holding quite an animated conversation with their boss. Amanda was clearly upset about something, and once she gestured wildly at them both. To my surprise, both men flinched a little as they cowered and took a step back from her, though she was substantially smaller than either one of them was.

Evidently she had a bite that matched her bark.

"What should we do?" Grace asked from the back seat. "Do we go talk to them when they're all together?"

"Hang on. Let's not rush it, okay? We should wait and see what happens first," Jake answered.

"I'll tell you what's going to happen," Grace said. "Those two men are being spanked pretty hard, and unless I miss my guess, they are about to slink off into the night."

Sure enough, three minutes later, the men left, and from the dim light coming from inside, I could see that they were both clearly happy to be getting away. What would Amanda do next, though? Would she leave as well, or would she go back inside? I got ready to follow her just in case, but to my relief, she returned to the shop instead.

Thirty seconds later, Jake had his hand on the car door. "Let's go. It's showtime, ladies."

Chapter 22

A minute later, Jake was knocking on the shop's front door, using that same booming voice again, but this time, Grace and I both were beside him. "Amanda, open up! We know that you're in there!" he said in his most officious voice.

Twenty seconds later, I whispered, "Why isn't she answering? Should I go around back to keep her from running away?"

"She's not like Kyle," Jake said to me in his normal voice, and then he knocked again. "This is your last warning!" Jake said loud enough to wake the neighborhood.

I was about to suggest a new approach when the door finally opened.

"It's you again," she said, resignation heavy in her voice. "What am I going to have to do to get you off my back?" Then she took in the fact that Grace and I were with Jake. "What did you do, bring your cheerleaders with you this time?"

"We're not cheerleaders," Grace said indignantly.

"My mistake," Amanda answered. "What do you want?"

"We need to talk about Rick Hastings," Jake said.

"Can't it wait until tomorrow?" Amanda asked him. "It's been a hard day, and I just want to go home."

"Sorry, but it needs to be right now. Amanda, we know that you were at Spirit Night in April Springs the night Rick was murdered." He dropped the fact as though it were a bomb, set to detonate on impact.

If it had any effect on Amanda, I couldn't see it. "I don't know what you're talking about."

"There's no use trying to deny it," I said. "We have proof."

"What proof?" she asked me, her gaze going instantly cold.

"It's a photograph of you with smeared makeup on," Grace said, clearly enjoying revealing the fact after the cheerleader crack.

Amanda knew that she'd been caught, at least attending the

festivities. How would she react to that? After a moment, she must have made up her mind to go along with it. "So what? I was driving through town and saw the activities. Some clown wanted to paint my face, so I thought, why not? It must have smudged a little when I rubbed my nose."

"Or it could have been from the sheet you were wearing when you killed Rick Hastings," I said. "We found that, too. DNA is a wonderful tool these days, don't you think?"

I wasn't sure how she'd react to the direct accusation, but when she simply shrugged in acquiescence, it was a surprise. "You might as well all come in. I'll tell you everything that really happened that night."

I noticed that Jake's gun was out as we all walked inside, but I never saw the thug waiting for us behind the door.

"Drop it, or I'll shoot," the man said, and Jake reluctantly did as he was told.

Chapter 23

"Just how stupid do you think I am?" Amanda asked as she retrieved Jake's gun from the floor, being careful to skirt around us. "I saw you pull up in that Jeep you drive, and I had a hunch that you were coming after me. That's why I sent Bruno here around the back so he could be waiting for you."

"Where's your other goon?" Jake asked as he looked around.

"Hey," Bruno said as he shoved the barrel of his gun into Jake's back. "Who are you calling a goon?"

"Bruno," Amanda snapped, and the thug took a step back. Evidently he was a pretty well-trained guerilla at that.

"I sent Hank to get some supplies," Amanda said.

"What kind of supplies do you need this time of night?" I asked.

"Oh, you know, the usual assortment of things: shovels, tarps, duct tape," she said with a smile. This was one wicked woman we were dealing with here. "In the meantime, we might as well spend our time wisely until he returns. Tell me, who else knows about this photograph?"

"The police have it right now," Jake said, "so it won't do you any good getting rid of us."

She laughed at that. "What a lovely bluff. You're very good at it, you know."

"What makes you think that he's bluffing?" Grace asked Amanda, her voice shaking a little with fear. And who could blame her? From where I was standing, we all had a sound reason to be afraid.

"Dear girl, if you had any real evidence against me, there would be more than the three of you knocking on my door. Some people might get a little suspicious after you all disappear, but nobody will be able to prove that I had anything to do with it."

This sociopath was serious! She'd already weighed the risk

of getting rid of us against being caught, and she had decided that it was her best course of action! We had to do something before Hank got back. We had the numbers on them, but we had no weapons, while they were both holding guns on us. Maybe it wasn't an ideal situation, but we couldn't just let ourselves be murdered without a fight.

The question was how best to attack. I glanced over at Jake, and I could almost see his mind working. Did he have a plan, or was he just going to spring on them without warning? I wished we had a way of coordinating our next move, but I didn't see any way that could happen.

Maybe if I stalled Amanda long enough, Jake would be able to come up with a way to let Grace and me know his intent.

"Why kill Rick at all, Amanda? I understand what it's like to be rejected, but it seems a little extreme to me."

Amanda shook her head in disgust. "I could probably take being thrown away, but for a donut girl? Are you kidding me? On the night I told Rick how I really felt, he claimed that he was seeing someone else, but when I pressed him on it, he said that she was just a distraction. Maybe she was, but she was still clearly more important to him than I was." I saw Amanda's hand tighten on the gun she was holding, and I wondered if I should push her any harder.

I was still thinking about how to deal with her when Grace spoke up. "I don't approve of what you did in any way, but I must say, putting on that sheet was a pretty clever disguise."

Amanda seemed pleased by the praise. "After I confronted Rick in the park, I was so angry! He pulled that stupid sheet over his head after he laughed at me, as if he were dismissing me as though I were some kind of pesky gnat! As I stormed away, I saw another sheet on the ground, and without thinking, I picked it up and put it on. He wasn't going to get away with treating me like that! I followed him over to the bonfire and stabbed him through the heart. My only regret is that he didn't know it was me the moment he died! He fell back into that pile of wood, I pulled the sheet off him, and then I dumped his and mine in the bushes nearby. I didn't figure anybody would tie them together with the crime, and I made my way back here."

The front door opened at that moment, and I knew that it was now or never.

I saw Jake brace for an all-out attack when I was shocked to see that instead of Hank, it was Kyle Creasy holding a hunting rifle!

As Kyle looked wildly around the inside of the garage, he shouted, "Where's Emma! What have you done with her!"

Bruno swung his gun around at the sound of Kyle's shouts, and Jake chose that moment and struck. He was grappling with the thug for the handgun just as Amanda shouted for everyone to put down their weapons. I was closest to her, but Grace wasn't that far away, and I'm proud to say that we tackled her together at nearly the exact same instant, as though we'd somehow coordinated our attack.

The gun went flying, clattering on the concrete floor, and I dove after it.

When I recovered it, I looked up to see that Amanda was now sitting up with Grace directly in front of her.

And then I noticed the steel blade in Amanda's hand, and how it was held tightly against my best friend's throat, ready to cut it at the slightest provocation.

Chapter 24

"Drop your weapons," Amanda rasped out, "or I swear I'll slit her throat right here and now."

"Will somebody please tell me where Emma is?" Kyle said loudly, confused by what had just transpired. The man was out of his mind. Had Jake's threats back at his place finally sent Kyle off the deep end? "Until someone tells me what's going on, I'm not putting my shotgun down. You can slit Grace's throat all you want to, for all I care."

"I care!" I shouted, though I still held the gun in my hands tightly. "Don't do it!"

"Then do as I say!" Amanda shouted.

At that moment, the door behind us opened again, and the second man we'd seen earlier arguing with Amanda came into the room. In his arms he carried all of the things she'd sent him to get, and that was probably the only thing that kept us alive at that moment.

"This woman killed Emma!" Grace shouted during the moment of confusion.

Kyle reacted instantly. His rifle exploded, and I saw both Grace and Amanda snap backwards.

Jake disarmed Kyle in an instant, but I barely noticed it.

When I rushed to Grace's side, I saw the blood. "Are you okay?" I asked her, my voice barely above a whisper now.

"I'm good," she said, still in a daze from what had just happened.

"Where exactly are you hurt?" I asked her, searching for a wound on her. The blood was making it impossible to tell exactly where she'd been hurt.

"This isn't my blood," she said shakily. "Kyle must have missed me entirely and hit Amanda."

We looked over at the killer and saw her lying a few feet away on the cold concrete floor grabbing her shoulder and moaning. "He shot me. That lunatic shot me."

"I should have killed you," Kyle said ferociously, and then

he launched himself at Amanda. "You took away my reason to live."

Jake neatly blocked him, and Grace approached the man carefully. "She's okay, Kyle. I was wrong. I made a mistake. Emma's fine."

"She's okay?" Kyle asked in clear disbelief. "Really? Are you sure?"

"I'm positive. Thank you for saving my life."

He completely ignored her thanks. "I want to see Emma."

Jake clamped a hand on his shoulder and moved him over Hank and Bruno. "Right now, you're not going to see anybody." He glanced at me. "Suzanne, did you get the knife, too?"

I started looking wildly around for it when Grace held it in the air, as though it were some kind of trophy. "Don't worry. I got it," she said.

"Don't let her move," Jake ordered.

Grace looked down at Amanda, who was clearly not in any shape to get up, let alone attack anyone else. "She's not going anywhere. I'll make sure of it," she said.

"Suzanne, call the police chief. He deserves to be in on this."

"I'm on it," I said, and I quickly dialed Stephen Grant's number.

When I told him what had happened, he had a hard time believing it at first, but by the time I finally convinced him that it was all true, I found myself talking to a dead cellphone.

Before we knew it, we were surrounded by the police, and Jake was finally able to turn over his charges and relinquish his guns.

It was over at last.

Chapter 25

"Good morning. What can I get for you, Chief Tyler?" I asked the next morning as our new police chief came into Donut Hearts just after we opened for business.

"I didn't think you'd be in today," the man said guardedly.

"This is my place of business. Where else would I be?"

"After hearing about what happened to you last night, I figured you might go ahead and take the day off," he said.

"If I did that, then where would the good citizens of April Springs get their breakfast?"

The new chief frowned a bit at my comment. "You're feeling pretty good about yourself right now, aren't you?"

"No more than most days," I said. "Why do you ask?"

"I heard all about what happened last night from *Officer* Grant," he said. It was pretty clear that Stephen Grant was about to have a few hard weeks under his new boss.

"You shouldn't hold anything that happened last night against him. He was just doing his job."

"It sounded more like you and your boyfriend were doing it for him."

"He's my fiancé, actually," I said, correcting him.

"Like it matters," the cop said. All signs of his earlier repentance were gone now, and I was faced with the same personality I'd seen the first time we'd spoken.

"It might not matter to you, but let me assure you that it matters a great deal to me," I said. I had intended to offer him a donut and a cup of coffee on the house for his first day of work even though he'd turned both down before, but I suddenly had a change of heart.

"You got lucky, Suzanne, whether you know it or not."

"Chief, I'm a firm believer that there's a little bit of luck in everything we do," I said.

"I'm not the chief yet," was the only answer he could come up with to that. "At least not for another two hours, anyway."

"Then if you don't mind me asking, exactly why are you here? You clearly aren't interested in anything that I have to offer," I said.

"I just wanted to set the record straight before I took over. I was forced to apologize under duress earlier, but once this job is mine, I'm going to run my department, and this town, the way I see fit. Is that understood?"

"Believe me when I tell you that I'd be happy if I never had to investigate another murder as long as I live," I said, and it was the complete and utter truth.

"That's good enough for me," he said with a smug smile.

I just couldn't let him walk away like that.

As he started to open the door, I added, "But if the need arises for me to ever do it again, nobody's going to stop me."

He hesitated for a moment, and then he kept walking.

Emma coughed lightly behind me. I hadn't even known that she'd been standing there.

"How much of that did you hear?" I asked her.

"Enough," she said. "You have to get George to change his mind before it's too late."

"Emma, I wouldn't do it, even if I could."

"Why not?"

"He has a right to run things as he sees fit. George can't handcuff him by making him tiptoe around me. I might not like his attitude, but since he's the police chief, I need to respect his wishes."

"Really?" she asked, clearly bewildered by my response.

"Well, at least up to a point," I said with a smile, and then we both laughed. "Now, don't you have more dishes to do?"

"If our doors are open, then there's work to be done," she said.

"Then I suggest that you do it," I said with a smile.

After she was back in the kitchen, I got a call from Jake.

"You're up early," I said.

"I just heard from the hospital. Amanda is going to be okay."

"Pardon me for not celebrating the news. After seeing that

knife blade at Grace's throat, I'm a little ambivalent about what happens to that woman from here on out."

"Understood. Oh, and they also ordered Kyle on a psychiatric hold. The man has some serious problems. Maybe this way he'll get some of the help that he needs."

"As long as he's out of Emma's life, that's all that I care about."

"Maybe not," Jake said.

"What do you mean?" His tone of voice had sent chills through me.

"He's fixated on someone else now."

"It's not me, is it?" I asked, fearing what his answer was going to be.

"No, as a matter of fact, it's Grace."

"Oh, no."

"Hopefully by the time he gets out, he'll be better," Jake said.

"In three days? I don't see how that's possible." I couldn't imagine the nightmare that Grace had been through with a blade at her throat, and now she was going to have to deal with this.

"I've got a hunch that's going to be extended indefinitely once they start talking to him," Jake said. "How's your morning been?"

"Well, the new police chief stopped by the donut shop and read me the riot act," I told him lightheartedly.

"Sure he did," Jake said, as though he were playing along with a nonexistent joke. "He didn't really, did he?"

"As a matter of fact, he did," I said.

"How did you respond?" Jake asked cautiously.

"I figure that he has the right not to want me to meddle in his murder cases," I admitted.

Jake breathed a sigh of relief. "Really?"

"He has the *right* to hope for it, but I didn't say that I was going to respect it," I added.

"That's more like the woman I know and love. Suzanne, if there's another murder on his watch, it's not going to be as easy for you as it was under Chief Martin."

"Whoever said that it was all that easy?" I asked. "Honestly, I don't want to talk about him anymore. What are we going to do after I close the donut shop today? Do you have any plans?"

"For the first time in my adult life, I don't have a single one," he said, and I could hear the smile in his voice. "How about you?"

"Between the two of us, I'm sure we can think of something," I said.

After we hung up, I marveled at how one person's obsession with another had taken a life, and how another's obsession had saved one. It was important to love, but just as important to be loved in return, and I was so happy to have that in my life again, or maybe for the first time ever, that I couldn't stop smiling for the rest of the day.

Jake surprised me by coming by just as I was closing up for the day.

"Hey, I didn't expect to see you here," I said as I brushed a stray strand of hair out of my face.

"What can I say? I missed you," he answered as he kissed me soundly right there in the shop in front of all the good folks of April Springs.

I laughed as I pulled away. "Already? That didn't take long."

"Listen, there's something we need to discuss," Jake said, now very serious.

"Okay," I said, wondering if he was going to tell me that he'd changed his mind and was going back to work for the state police, or maybe something even worse. Did he still want to marry me, or had he had a change of heart? "I'm listening."

"Last night I realized something, and I haven't been able to get it off my mind."

Oh, no. "What was that?" I asked noncommittally. "Are

you going back to the state police?"

"What? No. Never. This is about us."

"What about us?" I asked as my heart began trying to pound through my chest.

"Everything could have gone seven ways wrong last night, and all I could think about was the fact that we weren't married yet."

"Really?"

"Really. Did you have your heart set on a long engagement, or can we move things forward at a little more rapid pace?"

"Just how rapidly did you have in mind?" I asked him with a smile so broad that my cheeks hurt. This was the exact opposite of the news that I'd been worried about getting.

"Well, I'm free right now, you're just about finished with your work for the day. I know for a fact that the mayor's in his office for the entire afternoon. I figure that he can expedite the paperwork and we can be saying our vows before nightfall if you're up for it. What do you say to that? Oh, before you answer, this might sweeten the deal a little for you. I checked earlier, and we can get two tickets to Paris tonight if you say yes. We can be eating croissants as we stroll along the Seine tomorrow morning if that's what you want."

"Jake, are you offering me a honeymoon in Paris?" I asked him.

"I am."

I couldn't believe just how much I loved this man! "You don't have to bribe me with the trip of my dreams to get me to marry you."

He grinned at me. "Does that mean that you'll still marry me, and settle for an overnight stay in Union Square instead?"

"No, sir. We are going to Paris!"

He looked at me somberly for a moment before he spoke again. "Suzanne, is that a yes?"

"It is! Yes! Of course it's a yes! I'm in, Jake. I'm all in."

His smile was now broader than mine. "Then let's go round up your mother and Grace to be our witnesses, and let's do it."

And suddenly, in an instant, I knew that I had everything in the world that I'd ever truly wanted.

ORANGE DUNKERS

I got this idea from some treats my mother-in-law used to make at Christmas. They featured the candied oranges cut into cubes and added to an applesauce cake recipe. She baked hers in loaves, and we started making them in cupcake tins when I realized they would make a great baked donut! Making these adds a rich cinnamon taste to the air, and they are worth trying for that alone!

INGREDIENTS
WET
1-1 1/2 cups milk (2% or whole)
1 cup granulated sugar
1/2 stick butter, (1/4 cup), melted
3 egg yolks, beaten
2 tablespoons canola oil
1 tablespoon orange extract
Zest of one orange, fine

DRY
1/4 cup orange slice candies, cubed
1 teaspoon cinnamon
1 tablespoon baking powder
3-4 cups flour

DIRECTIONS

In a large mixing bowl, stir in the milk, sugar, melted butter, beaten egg yolks, canola oil, orange extract, and orange zest thoroughly until everything is well combined. In another bowl, stir together the cubed candy pieces, cinnamon, baking powder, and 3 cups of flour. After slowly adding the liquid, stir the mixture well. This will make a nice batter, but feel free to add more flour or milk to the mix in order to get a batter that easily scoops out on the edge of a tablespoon. Place in donut molds, or scoop out tablespoon-sized balls on a cookie sheet and bake at 375 degrees F for six to eight minutes, or until they are golden brown and spring back to the touch.

Yield: 8-10 Dunkers

DOODLE DROPS

These delightful little donut drops are easy to make, and they have the added benefit of being really tasty, particularly when it's cold outside. Not the fanciest donut we make by far, but we make these sometimes when time is of the essence, and particularly if there aren't any other treats in the house.

INGREDIENTS
WET
2 eggs, beaten
1/2 cup whole milk (2% will do in a pinch)
1/2 cup sugar, granulated white

DRY
1 1/2 cups flour (all-purpose unbleached is our first choice)
1 teaspoon nutmeg
1 teaspoon baking powder
1 dash of salt

DIRECTIONS

Beat the eggs together in a large mixing bowl, and then add the milk and sugar, stirring well. Set this aside, and in another bowl, sift together the flour, nutmeg, baking powder, and salt. Add the dry ingredients to the wet, stirring thoroughly. Use a small cookie scoop or two tablespoons to add the batter to 375 degree F canola oil, cooking for two to three minutes per side and turning the balls halfway through. These can be dusted with powdered sugar, iced, or slathered with jelly, jam, or my favorite, apple butter, or even better, pumpkin butter.

Yield: 10-12 drops

APPLE DROP TREATS

We first made these using apple cider, but we found it too limiting in our time frame, since cider isn't always available on our local store shelves. We've substituted apple juice instead on occasion, and now we enjoy these year round. For a stronger bite, substitute cider for the juice, and add some apple butter on top for a truly tasty treat! These can also be made adding small apple bits, but for a real treat, try using dried cranberries instead!

INGREDIENTS
WET
2 eggs, beaten
1 cup fresh apple juice (cider will do nicely, too)
1/4 cup brown sugar, light
1/4 cup sugar, white granulated

DRY
4 cups flour, unbleached all-purpose
1/2 teaspoon baking soda
1/2 teaspoon baking powder
1/2 teaspoon cinnamon
1/2 teaspoon nutmeg
Pinch of salt

FINAL ADDITION
1/4 cup butter, melted

DIRECTIONS

In a large mixing bowl, beat the eggs thoroughly, and then add the juice or cider. In a different bowl, combine the brown sugar and granulated sugar first, and then add the sugar mixture to the wet mix. After that's incorporated, take another bowl and sift together the flour, baking soda, baking powder, cinnamon, nutmeg, and salt. Incorporate the dry mix into the wet, and then add the melted butter last. The dough will most likely be sticky at this point, but work enough flour into the mixture to be able to scoop it out with a cookie scoop or two tablespoons. Fry the small round balls in hot canola oil at 375 degrees F for 3-4 minutes, turning them halfway through the process. These can be topped with powdered sugar, glazed with a simple icing, or simply dunked in the topping of your choice, from hot fudge to butterscotch to any of a number of jams.

Yield: 8-10 Drops

If you enjoy Jessica Beck Mysteries and you would like to be notified when the next book is being released, please send your email address to newreleases@jessicabeckmysteries.net. Your email address will not be shared, sold, bartered, traded, broadcast, or disclosed in any way. There will be no spam from us, just a friendly reminder when the latest book is being released.

Also, be sure to visit our website at jessicabeckmysteries.net for valuable information about Jessica's books.

22586310R00120

Made in the USA
San Bernardino, CA
12 July 2015